Blythe told Adam, 'and if you're honest with yourself, you don't want to marry me. Despite the fact that we slept together, we really don't like each other.'

'Maybe we could learn to like each other,' Adam stood. 'If we gave each other a chance and got to know each other, we might learn to be friends.'

'I doubt that will ever happen.'

'Why not?' Adam grinned. 'A few months ago neither of us would have believed we'd ever become lovers, and look what happened.'

Dear Reader,

Great holiday reading *is* Silhouette Desire®—but even if you're not going away this month, there's always July's scorching novels to make you feel better! Lounge in the garden or by the pool with our MAN OF THE MONTH, Bryan Willard, from Lass Small's *The Coffeepot Inn*—absolute bliss!

Follow Trenton Laroquette's search for the right woman in *The Bride Wore Tie-Dye* by Pamela Ingrahm, and don't miss Beverly Barton's *The Tender Trap*—where an unplanned pregnancy prompts an unexpected proposal!

Talented award-winning author Jennifer Greene has created another seductive story with the second of the Stanford Sisters in *Bachelor Mum*, and there's something a little bit different from Ashley Summers, *On Wings of Love*.

*The Loneliest Cowboy* is Pamela Macaluso's charming story where the hero meets up with an old flame he can't even remember, so he gets the surprise of his life when he hears her long-kept secret!

Enjoy!

The Editors

# The Tender Trap

# BEVERLY BARTON

™SILHOUETTE

*Desire*®

*Silhouette, Silhouette Desire and Colophon
are registered trademarks of Harlequin Books S.A.,
used under licence.*

*First published in Great Britain 1997
Silhouette Books, Eton House, 18-24 Paradise Road,
Richmond, Surrey TW9 1SR*

© Beverly Beaver 1997

ISBN 0 373 76047 7

22-9707

*Printed and bound in Great Britain
by Mackays of Chatham PLC, Chatham*

## BEVERLY BARTON

has been in love with romance since her grandfather gave her an illustrated book of *Beauty and the Beast*. An avid reader since childhood, she began writing at the age of nine, and wrote short stories, poetry, plays and novels throughout school and college. After marriage to her own 'hero' and the births of her daughter and son, she chose to be a full-time homemaker, a.k.a. wife, mother, friend and volunteer.

She returned to writing and since the release of her first Silhouette® book in 1990, she has won many awards. Beverly considers writing romances a real labour of love. Her stories come straight from the heart, and she hopes that all the strong and varied emotions she invests in her books will be felt by everyone who reads them.

### Other novels by Beverly Barton

*Silhouette Desire®*

Yankee Lover
Lucky in Love
Out of Danger
Sugar Hill
Talk of the Town
The Wanderer
Cameron
The Mother of My Child
Nothing But Trouble

With love and appreciation to a bright, funny, energetic
little ball of fire—my very special friend,
JoAnn Westfall. And a heartfelt *thank-you* to every
member of my Heart of Dixie RWA Chapter for
their continued support.

# One

---

Adam Wyatt was the sexiest man on earth. Blythe had thought so since the moment they met, nearly two years ago. Every time she saw him, the bottom dropped out of her stomach. Why was it that, of all the men she'd ever known, he was the one she couldn't stop fantasizing about? She could not keep herself from thinking about what it would be like to have him as her first lover.

Standing in the doorway leading to the patio, she watched Adam while he checked the outside area to make sure the caterer had cleared away everything. He turned, smiled and waved at her.

After the last guest had left, he had removed his jacket and tie. His wide shoulders strained against the pristine white shirt, and Blythe could see plainly the contours of his muscular, six-foot-two body. A heavy sprinkling of steel gray highlighted his thick mane of black hair, which was almost completely white along his sideburns and at his temples.

Adam was good-looking, in that very big, tough manly kind of way that made a woman's knees turn to jelly and her brain turn to mush. He was so drop-dead gorgeous few women could resist him.

Blythe quivered, then prayed the shudder hadn't been noticeable. Turning her back to him, she walked into the condo and took a deep, steadying breath. To most women Adam Wyatt was definitely irresistible, but *she* could resist him. She'd been doing just that for two years, and even if it killed her, she would go on resisting. He might be devastatingly handsome, charming and a self-made millionaire, but he was the wrong man for her.

Blythe was a modern woman—Adam was an old-fashioned man. They mixed like oil and water. Perhaps that was part of his attraction. He was everything she had always avoided in a man. He was the type she repeatedly told herself she didn't want. And that was the problem. She did want Adam—wanted him badly.

Giving in to her sexual urges in this case could mean disaster. Adam was too macho, too much the Me-Tarzan-You-Jane type. In that respect, he reminded her of her overbearing, domineering stepfather, and she had sworn long ago she'd never allow herself to fall for a man who'd try to dominate her.

Of course it wasn't as if Adam had been pursuing her. The exact opposite was true. Since their first meeting, when sparks had flown between them, he'd avoided her as much as possible. And she'd been glad. If she spent too much time with the man, there was always the chance she'd give in to her primitive feminine desire and throw caution to the wind.

Tears clouded Blythe's vision. She swallowed, then wiped her eyes. She had to stop this overemotional reaction to the day's events. The last thing she wanted was for Adam to catch her acting like some weak, weeping female.

She had tried not to cry, but despite her best efforts she'd greatly resembled a leaky faucet all afternoon. But then, it wasn't every day that a woman became a godmother.

Blythe lifted two empty champagne glasses onto the silver tray she held and placed the tray on top of the bar. Without thinking, she began picking up dirty plates and crumpled napkins from where they'd been left scattered around the living room in Adam's Brickyard Landing Marina condo.

"Hey, leave that stuff." Adam stepped inside through the sliding glass doors that opened onto his private brick patio overlooking the Tennessee River. "The housekeeper will take care of everything the caterers left when she gets here in the morning."

"Sure. I guess I'm so used to picking up after parties at my house, I didn't think."

Blythe glanced at Adam. Big, tall, rugged Adam, with his macho stance, his gruff voice and his slanting dark eyes.

Remember that you don't like him! Remember that he's not your type!

It had been mutual animosity at first sight when they'd met at the engagement party Adam had hosted for his lawyer, Craig Simpson, and Joy Daniels, Blythe's best friend. She supposed Adam was a nice enough man—if you liked his type. But she didn't like his type, and it had been apparent, from some of his remarks, that he was prejudiced against strong, independent career women.

"Everything went well, don't you think?" Leaving the sliding glass doors open behind him, Adam walked into the living room. "It was a new experience for me. I've never hosted a christening party before."

"We could have had the party at my apartment." Blythe had offered to give the christening party for her little goddaughter, but Adam had insisted on hosting the event. And Adam Wyatt always got his way.

"In that cracker box apartment of yours over on the southwest end of town?" Adam laughed, the sound a deep rumble from his broad chest. "You couldn't fit ten people into that tiny place, let alone the thirty Joy and Craig invited to Missy's christening. That's why we agreed to have the party here. Remember?" Falling into a navy blue leather chair, Adam stretched out his long legs in front of him as he raised his arms over his head and burrowed into the seat.

"You're right, I did agree for us to have the party here. I wanted today to be perfect. Joy is my best friend. Melissa is my goddaughter." Blythe clenched her teeth, narrowed her eyes and glared at Adam. "And you knew exactly how much having everything go exactly as we had planned meant to me."

"I figured you'd chew me out the minute we were alone," he said. "Just because I made a few minor changes to expedite matters, to simplify them a bit—"

"A few minor changes, my foot!" Blythe slammed her index finger down against her open palm. "First of all, you didn't use the caterer we had agreed to use." Down came her finger again. "Second, you changed the color scheme I chose." Smack. Her finger hitting her palm emphasized her aggravation. "Third—"

Adam threw up his hands in surrender. "Enough, woman! Enough."

"More than enough!" Blythe closed her mouth tightly, hoping to prevent herself from saying something she'd really regret.

"Look, I run a multimillion-dollar construction firm and have a large staff at my disposal. You don't. With your free time limited, I thought it more expedient to let my secretary handle the details of the christening party."

Blythe threw the handful of used napkins she'd gathered straight at him, but they missed the target and fell silently to the floor. "There, that should give your housekeeper something to complain about. The caterers I wanted to use would have cleaned up everything!"

"Pearl never complains." Adam grinned. "Unlike someone else I know who makes a habit of complaining."

Damn, he thought, how that little ball of fire irritated him and yet amused him at the same time. Blythe reminded him of a scratching, spitting kitten who was always on the defensive, always protecting herself, always afraid of being hurt.

"Do you want an apology?" Adam asked, figuring she was the type who'd enjoy seeing a man grovel.

"What good would an apology do? Make you feel better? Well, it won't change a thing. You bulldozed right over me, disregarding my wishes when you knew how important this day was to me."

"I thought everything went beautifully," he said.

"I suppose so. Everything went your way." Huffing loudly, she crossed her arms over her chest.

He'd had no choice but to host this party with Blythe, since Joy was her best friend, but dammit, his gut instincts had told him the two of them could never work together. He had known some stubborn, hardheaded, independent women in his time—and avoided them like the plague—but Blythe Elliott took the cake. She was the most argumentative female he'd ever run across, and he'd spent two years keeping his distance. But heaven help him, it hadn't been easy. Not when, despite everything, he wanted her—wanted her in his bed, crying out his name, begging him to pleasure her.

Crossing his arms behind his head, Adam closed his eyes and took a deep breath. Every time he spent more than two minutes with Blythe, he found himself wanting to either strangle her or kiss her. He wasn't sure which he wanted most. She had a chip on her shoulder when it came to him that he found hard to understand. He knew for a fact that she liked men, dated men and had men friends. But he was one man she didn't like, and that bothered him greatly. As a matter of fact, it bothered him a lot more than it should.

Blythe seemed to disapprove of him with a passion, and he simply couldn't figure out why. He'd never done anything to the woman. Hell, he'd given her a wide berth, staying out of her line of fire as much as possible, despite the fact that their best friends had married each other.

Opening his eyes, Adam sneaked a peek at Blythe and found her staring at him. "Look, I'm sorry if I upset you by slightly altering our plans. I honestly don't think you should object to an improvement over—"

"Let's just agree to disagree on this one." Glowering at him, Blythe sucked in her cheeks and blew out an exasperated breath. "And we'd better change the subject before I really lose my temper."

"Good idea." Shaking his head, Adam closed his eyes again and tried to relax. He didn't want to argue with Blythe, especially not today.

Blythe bent over, picked up the napkins she'd tossed at Adam and placed them on the end table. She decided she would be civil to him and end the day on as pleasant a note as possible.

"I thought it was wonderful that Joy and Craig christened my goddaughter, Melissa Blythe, after Joy's grandmother and me." Blythe hadn't been able to keep herself from crying during the christening ceremony. She couldn't remember a time in her life when she'd been so touched.

"Well, you could hardly expect them to name her Adam Tobias Maximillian Wyatt."

Blythe stared at Adam, trying hard to keep from smiling. The effort failed. "Good grief, is that really your name? Adam Tobias Maximillian Wyatt?"

Blythe burst into laughter. Groaning, Adam opened his eyes and stared at her. He shot out of his chair and playfully grabbed her by the shoulders. Smiling, he shook her gently. "I can't believe I told you. Forget you ever heard that. Okay?"

She trembled with laughter, her body quivering beneath his fingertips. Damn, but she was tiny, her bones so very fragile. He doubted she weighed much more than a hundred pounds soaking wet. She had to be a foot shorter than he was; the top of her head struck him midchest. If he kissed her, he'd have to pick her up to reach her mouth.

Hell, he couldn't let himself think about kissing her. She was the last woman on earth he should want. But he did want—had wanted her from the first moment he'd seen her in a body-hugging purple dress that accentuated every curve of her petite body. He'd spent the whole night of Craig and Joy's engagement party struggling to control his arousal.

The moment Adam touched her, Blythe gazed up into his dark eyes. He looked at her intensely. What was he thinking? If she didn't know better, she'd swear he wanted to kiss her.

Dropping his hands from Blythe's shoulders, Adam took a step backward. Blythe sucked in a deep breath. A loud rumble of thunder shattered the uneasy silence. A zigzag of ragged lightning ripped through the cloudy, gray evening sky.

"I guess I'd better get going since you don't need me to hang around and help you clean up." Blythe backed away from Adam, bumping into the edge of an end table.

Heavy drops of rain hit the patio. The wind blew the dampness inside through the open doors. Turning quickly, Adam rushed to shut out the rain.

"You might want to wait around until this summer storm passes," he said. "It probably won't last long. They never do."

She didn't want to stay. Not one minute longer. Not alone with Adam Wyatt. She knew his reputation with women. Every time she saw him, he had a different voluptuous beauty on his arm.

So what are you worried about, Blythe? she asked herself. Adam Wyatt wouldn't touch you with a ten-foot pole. You're hardly his type any more than he's yours. He likes tall, big-boobed, helpless, brainless lovelies who simper and gush and cling to him like ivy to a brick wall.

"Yeah, you're right," Blythe said. "No use getting soaked." She sat down on the leather sofa, perching her petite body tensely on the edge.

"Want something to drink?" he asked, eyeing the bar. "I could use something stronger than champagne myself."

"Nothing for me. Thanks." Blythe glanced outside. The rain poured from the sky. Suddenly the world shook with thunder. She gasped, her body trembling involuntarily.

"Are you afraid of storms?" Adam chuckled as he rounded the bar and lifted a bottle of bourbon from a low shelf.

"No. Not really. I just don't like them."

She hated storms, but that fact was none of Adam's business. Being afraid of thunder and lightning could be seen as a weakness, a female weakness. Her stepfather had made fun of her mother's fear of storms, telling her what a silly woman she was and what a good thing it was that he was around to take care of her since she couldn't take care of herself.

Raymond Harold had been a big, handsome man, totally masculine in every way. He had taught Blythe never to trust men, especially big, macho men who liked to *take care* of women. She'd watched her lovely, kind, intelligent mother dominated and manipulated. No man would ever subjugate her. No man would ever turn her into "the little woman" and convince her she wasn't capable of making her own decisions.

Adam carried his glass of bourbon with him, sat down on the sofa beside Blythe and took a sip of the mellow liquor. She scooted as far away from him as she could without getting up.

"What do you think I'm going to do, jump on you?" He sloshed the bourbon around inside the glass, then took a hefty swallow, shaking his head and blowing when the liquid blazed a trail down his throat and into his stomach.

"I understand you have that sort of reputation." Blythe glared at him, issuing him a challenge without realizing what she was doing.

Adam set his drink down on the glass-and-brass coffee table, then turned to face Blythe, laying his hand across the back of the sofa and lifting his right knee onto the cushion. "Ms. Elliott, you don't have a thing to worry about. When I take a woman, I want her to be just that—a woman. And I want her willing. No, I want her more than willing. I want her begging for it."

Blythe cursed the blush she felt spreading up her neck and onto her face. She was supposed to be a woman of the world, dammit. She had dated practically every unattached man in north Alabama, and found them all lacking in one way or another. None of the guys she dated wanted to admit that he'd been the first one she had refused to sleep with, so no one, except Joy, knew that Blythe Alana Elliott was a twenty-eight-year-old virgin.

Clutching the thickly padded sofa arm with her hand, Blythe looked at Adam. "For the life of me, I can't figure out why Joy chose you to be Melissa's godfather. If anything were to happen to Joy and Craig, you'd make the worst possible father substitute in the world."

"And you'd make a great mother, I suppose?"

"I'd certainly try to be a good mother." Blythe's sculptured lavender nails bit into the leather as she squeezed the sofa arm tightly. "Since I'm not married, I can't say that motherhood is something I've thought about very much...until Joy got pregnant. I adore Missy. She'd never want for love and attention from me."

"Well, believe me, I haven't given fatherhood a thought since my divorce, but if that little girl ever needed me, I'd be there for her."

"No little girl should be raised by a man like you!" Blythe jumped up off the couch, intending to go into the bedroom, where she'd deposited her purse when she'd arrived before the party started.

Adam stood, followed her across the living room and into his downstairs bedroom. Stopping abruptly in the doorway, Blythe glanced over her shoulder.

"What do you want?" she asked.

"Just what kind of man do you think I am?"

Adam didn't know why her accusation had stung so badly. Maybe it was because once he had wanted a child of his own desperately. He and Lynn had tried for two years of their five-year marriage, but his wife had never gotten pregnant. Just when he had agreed for them to seek medical advice, he had discovered Lynn's infidelity. She hadn't married her lover, but she had eventually remarried, finished law school and was now a successful attorney in Birmingham.

He supposed he had loved Lynn once, when they'd first married and he'd thought she wanted nothing more than to be his wife and the mother of his children. But she hadn't been satisfied with their comfortable life—a life he had worked hard to give her.

A simple explanation for the demise of their marriage would be to say that they grew apart or grew in different directions. But the way Adam saw it, he had given in to her wants and wishes time and time again. He had compromised his ideals for her, had accepted the fact she wanted a career and had supported her efforts. He'd done everything possible to save their faltering relationship, but the one thing he couldn't compromise on was fidelity. She'd taken a lover. And Adam had never forgiven her.

Turning slowly to face him, Blythe gazed up into Adam's stern face, into his stormy brown eyes, and shivered.

"I think you're a big, macho stud who reaches out and takes what he wants. You believe women have one purpose. You'd like to see us all kept barefoot and pregnant."

Heat rose up his neck and into his face. How dare this little snip of woman accuse him of being such a jerk. What did she know about him, about the kind of man he was?

"What is it with you?" Adam asked, moving toward Blythe slowly, forcing her to confront him face-to-face. "I've never done a damned thing to you, but you attack me every time we meet."

"I know your type. You're all alike. All of you. Keep a woman in her place. Tell her what she can and can't do. Make all her decisions for her, and do it all in the name of love. Your wife probably divorced you because she couldn't endure another day of being totally dominated." Blythe backed into the bedroom, cautiously moving away from the big man whose facial expression told her he was on the verge of exploding. "I'm going to get my purse and leave. Occasionally I find your macho man act amusing, but not now. I'm too tired for another sparring match."

Adam overtook her just as she backed into his king-size bed, the slight jar of her legs against the mattress making her unsteady on her feet. He grabbed her by the shoulders. Thunder boomed. The windows rattled. Blythe cried out, tears filling her eyes. Why did she keep crying? It wasn't like her to be this emotional over nothing. Admit it, she told herself, Adam Wyatt has you running scared. You want him so bad you can taste it, but you know falling for him would be the biggest mistake of your life. Balling her hands into fists, she longed to strike out at Adam, hoping that by fighting him she could overcome the temptation to throw herself into his arms.

Tightening his hold on her shoulders, he shook her. "Where the hell did you get those ridiculous ideas about my ex-wife and me?"

"I figured it out on my own." Blythe tried to free herself from his hold, then ceased struggling and swatted at her tearstained face. "I've had more than enough of you for one day. Let go of me. I want to leave."

"Calm down," he told her. "You can't go out in the rain, upset and crying. You're liable to have a wreck."

Swallowing her tears, Blythe jerked away from Adam and tried to turn around, only to be confronted by the king-size black metal bed. She could feel Adam directly behind her, could feel his strength and power. Dear God, she had to get away from him, get away from the way he made her feel.

"Blythe?" His voice dropped to a deep baritone, the sound echoing in the stillness of the room.

She trembled when he placed his hands on her shoulders, slowly turning her to face him. She hung her head, avoiding eye contact.

"Who the hell made you dislike men so much, and me in particular?" It became apparent to Adam that somewhere along the way, some man had done a number on Blythe Elliott. What other explanation could there be for her actions?

"Not all men—just overbearing macho ones like you. My stepfather made my mother his slave. Wouldn't let her have a career. She had no life of her own, no income, no way to escape him. He made her totally dependent on him and loved having her beg him for every..." Blythe gulped down her anger at the same time she tried to wipe the tears from her eyes. Her hand trembled. "Raymond was a real son of a bitch!"

Adam reached down, touching her cheeks with his fingertips, brushing away the dampness of her tears. "Do I remind you of your stepfather?"

"Yes!" Blythe shook her head. "No, not really. It's just that you're a big man, very masculine, very handsome, and...and women seem to adore you. You're an old-fashioned, macho guy. Raymond was like that."

Adam couldn't remember a time in his life when he'd felt as protective of anyone as he did Blythe at this precise moment. He wanted to gather her into his arms, hold and comfort her, make her feel safe and secure. "Don't confuse me with your stepfather. All men aren't bastards. Surely you've discovered that fact by now. It's not like there haven't been men in your—"

Another loud blast of thunder drowned out the sound of Adam's voice. Gasping, Blythe grabbed Adam around the waist, clinging to him.

He stroked her short hair, the dark auburn strands beneath his hand like heavy, cinnamon silk to the touch. "It's all right, babe. I'm here. I'll take care of you."

Blythe froze the moment she heard his declaration. Glaring at him, she eased her arms from around his waist and punched him in the chest with her finger. "I don't *need* anyone to take care of me!"

"We all need somebody to take care of us," Adam said. "Women need men. Men need women. Needing someone isn't a weakness, you know. A real woman knows how to give and take."

She lifted her hands, gripping the lapels of his jacket, staring up at him, her eyes pleading with him—she did need something from him, but Adam wasn't sure what.

Slowly, he cradled the back of her head with his palm, roaming his other hand down her neck, bringing her body closer to his. He looked into her green-flecked hazel eyes and was lost. Diamond teardrops glistened in her thick reddish brown lashes. Her full, pouty lips opened slightly as she breathed in and out. The sprinkling of tiny freckles across her nose beckoned him to kiss each pale copper dot.

Blythe Elliott was utterly enchanting.

Hell, what was he thinking? What was he doing? Loosening his hold on her, Adam took a step backward.

"Adam?" Blythe felt lost without him, without the touch of his fingers in her hair, the support of his hand on her back. She didn't want him to release her. She'd be alone again. So very alone.

"I'll drive you home." He turned to leave the room. "I'll get someone to bring your car over to your apartment in the morning."

Although he had his back to her, Blythe nodded her head. She stood frozen to the spot by the bed for a few minutes, waiting while Adam walked out into the hall. She picked up her purse, hung it over her shoulder and followed him.

"I can drive myself home." She couldn't understand the overwhelming urge she had to ask him if she could stay with him. *I don't want to go, Adam. I want to stay here with you. I want you to...*

"If you drive yourself, I'll worry about you," he said.

When they neared the front door, Adam flipped the light switch, throwing the room into semidarkness. Only the fluorescent light over the bar area remained on. He opened the door, stood to one side and waited for Blythe. She walked outside, hesitating momentarily at the wrought iron gate that opened directly onto the private drive behind the condos. He placed his hand on the small of her back.

Then he realized, too late, that he shouldn't have touched her. He didn't want her to leave. He wanted her to stay, to spend the night in his arms.

"You don't have to leave, you know." He spread his fingers open wide, touching her lower back and the upper curve of her buttocks. "You could stay."

Turning slowly, she stared up at him and saw the undisguised raw passion in his brown eyes, eyes so dark and deep they appeared black. "Do you want me to stay?"

"Yes, I want you to stay." He growled the words.

She swallowed hard, wondering if she'd lost her mind. "This is crazy, Adam. We're crazy. You want me to stay, and . . . I want to stay."

Sweeping her up into his arms, he lowered his head and claimed her lips in a kiss of total possession. She clung to him, returning the kiss with eagerness. Taking her back inside his condo, he closed the door behind them and shut out the reality both of them had momentarily forgotten.

He carried her into his dark bedroom. A faint, gray light shimmered in through the floor-to-ceiling windows. Shadows fell across the gold-and-black striped coverlet, wavered on the golden cream-colored wall and encompassed the room in a seductive quiet.

Adam laid Blythe down on the bed, then stood over her, staring at her. Suddenly she felt very small and totally helpless.

"Adam, maybe we're—" She started to say that maybe they were making a mistake, a big mistake, but before she could finish the sentence, he leaned over and kissed her. His mouth was hard and hot and moist.

She returned the kiss, draping her arms around him and trying to drag his body onto hers. Even though she had never made love with a man, she wasn't totally inexperienced. She'd felt passion before, had known what it was like to want a man, but nothing had prepared her for this uncontrollable need.

He came down over her, kissing her until she couldn't breathe, until she thought she'd die from the pleasure of being so completely consumed. He slipped his big hand beneath her, seeking and finding the zipper pull at the back of her dress. Easing open her lavender linen dress, he lifted her body just enough to insert his hand inside the waistband of her lace half-slip.

When he delved his hand inside her lavender bikini panties and made contact with her naked buttocks, Blythe
groaned against his marauding lips. He nuzzled the side of
her neck and whispered her name. She trembled. He sighed.

He brought her hand to his shirt, encouraging her to un-
button it. Slowly, hesitantly at first, she began to undress
him while he tugged her dress off her shoulders and down
to her waist. All the while, he kept touching her, kissing her,
talking to her.

"You're so little, babe. So delicately made. So fragile. I
don't want to hurt you."

She threw his shirt on the floor, then drew in a deep
breath when she looked at his wide, naked chest. Heavily
muscled, covered with dark curling hair, his body beckoned her touch.

"You're beautiful," she said, then laid her hand on his
washboard-lean stomach.

Adam sucked in his breath. His sex hardened. He lifted
himself up and off the bed, then divested himself of the remainder of his clothes.

Blythe had never seen a fully aroused man, but she didn't
think all men looked like Adam Wyatt. He was big, deeply
tanned, powerfully built and overwhelmingly male. She
swallowed hard, and for one split second wondered if she
was woman enough for such a man.

But the moment he lay down beside her and took her in
his arms, all doubts and uncertainties vanished like snow
melting in the warm sun.

"I want to look at you," he told her when he unhooked
the front closure of her lavender bra.

She nodded her head, wishing she was more experienced.
How long was it going to take him to figure out that this was
her first time? And if he did, would he stop? If he called a
halt to things now, she didn't think she could bear it.

He spread the bra apart and gazed down at her small,
firm breasts. "Perfect," he said, then covered them with his
hands, gently kneading them, circling her nipples with his
palms.

She shivered. Her femininity tightened. Lowering his mouth, he teased one nipple while he stroked its mate to a point between his thumb and forefinger. Lifting her hips off the bed, she slid her arms around his waist and pressed herself intimately against him.

His mouth and hands moved over her swiftly, taking a speedy inventory of every luscious inch from face to toes, as he discarded the remainder of her clothes. Blythe succumbed to her own desire to fondle him, to discover the secrets of his manhood. They explored each other with a hunger neither could deny nor restrain. The fever burning hot inside them blazed out of control.

"I can't wait." He panted the words against her breast. "Next time, we'll go slower. I promise."

Blythe ached with such a wild need, she made no protest when he mounted her and sought entrance into her body. She was surrounded by him. By the bulk of his massive shoulders. By the aura of masculine power he possessed. By his hot, musky smell, his hypnotizing black eyes and the mesmerizing tone of his deep voice.

"I want you," was all she could say.

She was warm and moist and willing, her arms holding him close, yet her body resisted his invasion. She was tight, so very tight. And he was on the verge of exploding. He had wanted her so badly, for so long, that being inside her was his only goal in life at this precise moment.

Lifting her hips, he thrust into her, then stopped when he realized the truth. He'd thought she was experienced, that she'd had a legion of lovers.

A hot, searing pain pierced her. Blythe gasped, tears filling her eyes. The pain didn't matter. Nothing mattered, except making love with Adam.

He partially withdrew from her. "Why didn't you tell me, babe?"

She bit her bottom lip, then swallowed her tears and reached up to caress his face. "Because I wanted you, and I was afraid that if you knew, you—"

He silenced her with a kiss, plunging his tongue into her mouth at the same moment he delved deeply into her body, taking her completely. She groaned into his mouth, wanting the discomfort to end, but not wanting him to stop.

He couldn't make it last, couldn't take the time she needed, couldn't give her complete pleasure this time. He took her quickly, wild with the need. His climax rocketed through him like blasts of dynamite. When the last aftershock subsided, he slid to her side, wrapped her in his arms and kissed her gently.

Cuddling against him, she felt joyous at having given Adam such intense pleasure, and yet she felt bereft, wanting to experience that same earth-shattering ecstasy.

"The next time will be for you. All for you," he said. "I was too hungry for you, wanted you too desperately to make it perfect."

He caressed her hip while they lay together in each other's arms. He thought about all the things he was going to do to her, all the wonderful things he was going to teach her. The first time, he'd lost control. The first time, she'd been a virgin.

Adam jerked upright in bed. Blythe laid her hand on his back. "What's wrong?" she asked. "Are you all right?"

The realization that he hadn't used a condom hit him square in the gut. How the hell could he have been so stupid? He always took the proper precaution. Not once since his divorce had he made love to a woman without protection.

"I'm okay," he said, lying down beside her and pulling her into his arms. "Everything's fine."

When he made love to her again—and he intended to make love to her all night—he'd make sure he didn't take any more chances.

# Two

——

"Mr. Wyatt, there's a Ms. Blythe Elliott here to see you, sir." Sandra Pennington's voice sounded a bit shaky, and that was unusual for the formidable middle-aged woman who'd been Adam's secretary for the past ten years. "She insists on seeing you immediately."

Blythe Elliott? Here? At his office? Insisting on seeing him? Would wonders never cease?

Adam's stomach tightened into knots. What was she doing here? They hadn't been together in over two months—not since the night they'd both lost their senses and made love like a couple of wild animals who couldn't get enough of each other.

Just the memory of that night aroused Adam. And the last thing he wanted was to get hot and bothered remembering what it had been like becoming Blythe's first lover. Damn, he'd thought she was experienced, and he'd gotten the surprise of his life.

When he'd awakened the next morning, Blythe was gone, only the scent of her remained in his bed. He'd tried calling her. She'd hung up on him time and time again. He'd gone to her apartment. She'd slammed the door in his face. He'd cornered her at her Petals Plus florist, only to be told that she hated him and never wanted to see him again.

It had taken him more than one try before he finally got the picture. Whatever had happened between them the night of little Melissa Simpson's christening had been an aberration, a fluke, a chance happening. Adam had accepted that fact and moved on with his life. At least he'd tried to move on. He had wined and dined several lovely ladies over the last two months, but every time the mood turned serious, he'd see a pair of big hazel eyes looking up at him, he'd hear those sweet little sounds of pleasure Blythe had made when he'd taken her, and he'd feel those small, fragile bones, that soft, sleek freckled flesh he'd caressed the whole night through.

"Tell Ms. Elliott to come in."

Should he stand? Should he remain seated? Should he be friendly or act nonchalant? Should he ask why she was paying him a visit or just say it was good to see her?

Remaining seated, he leaned over his desk and rested his clasped hands in front of him.

She swept into the office like a tiny whirlwind, her straw bag clutched to her side, her chin tilted defiantly, her gaze riveted directly to his face.

Whatever her reason for coming to his office, Adam's gut instincts told him this was no social call. It was a confrontation.

Blythe looked even prettier than he remembered. Her short cinnamon red hair shone with a healthy vibrance. Her skin had tanned a rich gold, her freckles darkened to muted copper dots on her nose, cheeks and shoulders. She wore a yellow miniskirt, a matching peach-and-yellow polka-dot blouse and a pair of small gold hoops in her ears.

"If I'm interrupting something, I apologize," she said. "I wouldn't be here if it wasn't important."

"Sit down, Blythe. Tell me why you're here." Of all the women he'd known over the years, why was this little hellion the only one he'd been unable to walk away from and forget? Because she'd been a virgin? Because he'd carelessly forgotten to use protection the first time they'd made love?

She sat tensely on the edge of the white leather-and-chrome chair to the left of Adam's huge, black metal desk. Easing her purse into her lap, she clutched it as if it were a lifeline.

"Would you like some coffee? Or tea? A soft drink?" What was wrong with her? he wondered. Why was she so nervous?

"No, nothing. Thanks."

"How have you been?" he asked.

"I've been just fine. How about you?"

"No complaints," he said. "Look, it isn't that I'm not glad to see you, but your visit comes as quite a surprise. Two months ago, you refused to see me. You wouldn't even talk to me on the phone. I have to admit that I'm curious as to why you're here today."

Oh, this was going to be more difficult than she'd thought. Adam was being nice. Not too nice, but nice enough. After the way she'd treated him, he had every right not to speak to her. But what should she have done? Good grief, they had made a monumental mistake—the biggest mistake of her life. She still didn't know what had come over her that evening at Adam's condo. Why, after resisting temptation for two years, had she given in that night? One minute they'd been arguing and she'd disliked everything his powerful, macho image represented and the next thing she knew she was practically begging him to make love to her. One minute she'd wanted to run from him, and the next minute she couldn't get close enough.

"I want you to know that I don't hold you responsible." Blythe lowered her eyes, not able to continue looking directly at Adam. "It was my fault. I should have known better." She stood up. Her purse fell to the floor. "I did know better, but I'd never felt anything so powerful before. I just didn't know how to handle wanting someone so much."

Adam shoved back his chair and stood. "Why should we rehash that night now, after two months, when you've refused to see me or speak to me before today?"

Bending over, she picked up her bag and flung it in the chair she'd just vacated, then turned to face him. He seemed so distant, so in control, so much the Adam Wyatt she'd known and avoided for two years. "I'm not here to discuss what happened a couple of months ago. Well, in a way, I am. That is to say, the reason I'm here is to tell you that, well, after we . . . after we—"

"Made love," Adam said.

"Yes, after we made love, I knew you would regret it as much as I did, and I realized that you'd feel responsible, even guilty because I'd been a . . . well, I'd been—"

"The word is *virgin,* babe. You were a virgin."

"Yes, well, I felt there was no point in our blaming ourselves for something that wasn't your fault or mine. It just happened."

"It happened three times." The statement was out of his mouth before he could stop himself from speaking. Damn! What was the point of reminding her? Of reminding himself?

Blythe covered her face with her hands. Blowing out a loud breath, she closed her eyes and ran her fingers through her hair. "This isn't easy for me. Okay? It's taken all the courage I could muster to come here today to tell you."

"To tell me what?" he asked. "That you don't blame me for our night of passion two months ago?"

"No, I don't blame you. I blame myself." Blythe balled her hands into fists at her sides. "I don't expect you to do anything. And I'm not asking for anything. I just thought you had a right to know."

Adam glared at her, not quite sure what the hell she was talking about, but getting a sinking feeling in his stomach. "You thought I had a right to know what?"

"I'm pregnant!" There, she'd said it. The worst was over. Or so she thought.

"You're *what?*"

Adam rounded his desk so quickly that Blythe didn't have a chance to get away from him before he grabbed her by the shoulders, his fierce grip jerking her forward. He stared at her. Her eyes opened wide as she bit down on her bottom lip.

"You're what?" he repeated.

"I'm pregnant."

She was pregnant! No, it wasn't possible. Who was he kidding? Of course it was possible.

He ran his hands down her arms, clasping her wrists with his fingers. "I'm sorry, Blythe. I never meant for this to happen."

She shrugged, tilting her head to one side, a tentative smile quivering on her lips. "I know. I told you that I don't blame you."

"You should!" Releasing his hold on her, he turned away, slamming his big fists down on top of his desk. "In all the years since my divorce, I've never made love to a woman without using protection. Not once. Not until that night. With you. The first time."

"I didn't use anything, either," Blythe said, wanting to touch Adam's back, waiting to reach out and place her hand on his massive shoulders. "I mean, I wasn't on the Pill or anything."

Lifting his clenched fists, he turned and braced his hip on the edge of the desk. "Well, we can't go back and change what happened. God knows I would if I could. We've got to deal with the consequences, to make decisions about how we're going to handle this situation."

Blythe didn't know what she had expected him to say when she told him. Deny that he was the father? Tell her it was her problem? Or had she secretly hoped he'd be happy, that he'd lift her in his arms, kiss her and tell her he loved her and wanted their child?

But Adam didn't love her any more than she loved him. If he could go back and change what had happened, he would. He'd just said so himself. And if she could go back to that night, what would she do? Unconsciously, she slid her hand down the front of her skirt, her open palm covering her stomach.

"I suppose you've considered all the options," Adam said. Dear God, what would he do if she said she planned to have an abortion? He'd tell her she couldn't, that he didn't want her to destroy the child they had created together.

"Yes, I discussed options with my doctor and with Joy."

"You told Joy? She and Craig know?"

"I told Joy yesterday. She's the one who convinced me to come here today and tell you. She promised not to say anything to Craig until after I'd talked to you."

"Have you made a decision?" He knew *he* had already made a decision about the baby. It didn't require any lengthy soul-searching. He'd gotten Blythe pregnant. She was carrying his child. He'd marry her. That was the only honorable thing to do.

"I decided against having an abortion."

Relief spread through Adam. His tight muscles relaxed. "Good. I wouldn't want you to do that."

Closing her eyes, Blythe said a silent prayer of thanks that he hadn't expected her to dispose of their *mistake*.

"My doctor and I discussed the possibility of giving the baby up for adoption." Dr. Meyers had tried to discuss adoption with her, but she'd adamantly refused. She had no intention of giving away her child.

Would she give his child to perfect strangers? Dammit, he wouldn't let her! If Adam had to, he'd do as his father had done and raise the child by himself. "Adoption? Don't even consider giving away my child."

"I didn't consider it. Not really. I'm going to have my baby and I'm going to keep her." Blythe had decided that the baby was a girl. She couldn't imagine herself raising a boy—some rough and rowdy little black-eyed boy who'd grow up to look just like Adam.

Adam let out the breath he'd been holding. "You're going to keep the baby?"

"I came here to tell you because Joy pointed out the fact that, as the father, you did have a right to know." Glancing away from Adam, Blythe reached into the chair and picked up her purse. "I don't expect you to get involved. I'm not here asking for any kind of support."

"Just what are you trying to say?" Standing, he grabbed her by the arm as she turned from him. "You waltz in here and tell me that you're going to have my child, but you don't expect me to get involved. Well, babe, you'd better think again. That's my baby, too." He looked directly at Blythe's flat stomach, his fingers itching to reach out and touch her, to lay a protective hand over his child.

"You want to be involved?" She stared at him, not sure she had heard him correctly.

"Damn right, I do."

"How is that possible, Adam? I don't think there's any way you and I can share a child."

"Well, we'd better figure out a way, hadn't we?"

She gasped when he laid his hand across her stomach. The touch was so innocent and yet at the same time so compellingly intimate.

*His child.* He'd given this woman his baby—and she wanted it. He smiled, thinking about Blythe referring to their baby as her. A daughter. His daughter. He liked the sound of that. *His daughter.*

"In what . . . seven months . . . our child will be a reality? I don't think we should waste time on a big, fancy affair, do you? Something simple, but elegant. Craig can stand up for me and Joy can be your matron of honor."

What? Surely she had misunderstood what he'd said. It sounded as if he were planning a wedding. "Do you expect me to marry you?"

"Of course I do. Our child isn't going to come into this world a bastard, her mother and father unmarried."

"But—but we can't get married."

"Why not?"

"We don't love each other. We don't even like each other very much." Blythe eased away from Adam's possessive hand, removing her body from his reach. "Until the night we... er...made love, we couldn't be in the same room together without getting into an argument."

"We don't argue when we're in bed together. All we do is—"

"Don't say it! I know what happened that night. We both went crazy, but I'm not crazy now, and I know I can't marry you. It would be wrong."

"It would be wrong not to marry. Can't you see? Even if you and I aren't in love, even if we have our differences, we owe it to our child to get married. And we owe it to ourselves. After all, Decatur is a pretty old-fashioned Southern town, you know, and we both have reputations to uphold. Hell, you coach a girls' softball team, don't you? And I'm on the board of education."

"I don't like your type of man, Adam. Even if we both lose our reputations, it would be better than trying to live together. We'd wind up killing each other."

"You didn't dislike me the night you conceived my child. You gave a good impression of a woman who liked everything about me." Adam laughed when he heard her gasp.

"That's typical of your type, reminding me of what a fool I was. I was very emotional that evening. I'd just become a godmother. Joy named her baby after me, and I was all emotional and everything. Then the thunderstorm blew up... and... and I... I—"

"Acted like a woman. A real woman. Soft and vulnerable and loving."

"I made the mistake of falling right into your big, strong arms. You were...were...irresistible, and for the first time, I gave in to my desires. And just look what happened!" Determined not to cry, Blythe clamped her teeth tightly together.

Adam reached out for her; she backed farther away from him. "You want me to take the blame?" he asked. "You want me to say it was my fault? All right, it was my fault. I shouldn't have made love to you. I knew how emotional you were, how vulnerable. But dammit, Blythe, I didn't know you'd never been with a man. I thought you'd had sex with all those idiots you dated."

"Well, I hadn't. And why I couldn't resist you, I'll never know."

Adam grinned. "You couldn't resist me, huh?"

She flung her purse at him. It bounced off his chest and hit the floor. Oh, damn! Why had she just admitted that she hadn't been able to resist him that night? She was such a fool. "Ooo...hhh!"

"We should have an exciting marriage." Reaching down, Adam picked up her purse and held it out to her. "We can fight all day and make love all night."

Blythe grabbed her purse. "I am not going to marry you."

"If you think I'm suggesting a love match, then stop worrying." Adam realized he'd have to play things just right or Blythe would walk out of his office and out of his life, taking his child with her.

Blythe held her purse against her chest, her arms criss-crossed at her waist. "What are you suggesting?"

"I'm suggesting that we get married to give our baby legitimacy, to give *her* two parents, and to maintain our good reputations. We both have a lot to lose as unwed parents." He watched Blythe as she considered what he'd said. She was weakening just a little. All he had to do was continue persuading her. "When we get married, we can have separate bedrooms, if that's what you want."

"What kind of marriage would that be?"

"A marriage in name only. For the sake of the baby. After she... or he... is born, we can get an amicable divorce and share joint custody of our child. That shouldn't be any problem."

"No, that shouldn't be any problem," she mumbled. "Would everybody know... I mean would we have to tell people that..."

"Nobody needs to know anything about our personal business. If you want to tell Joy, it would be all right with me."

"I don't know. I didn't come here expecting you to propose marriage." *Liar!* her conscience screamed at her. *Deep down, in your heart of hearts, you came here to Adam hoping he'd find a way to make everything all right. First you break your own cardinal rule about not having sex, then you get yourself pregnant, and now you're considering marrying the big jerk.*

"Think about it. Talk to Joy." Adam glanced down at his watch. "It's ten-thirty. Take all day. I'll pick you up for dinner tonight and we'll discuss the situation and make plans."

"I guess it wouldn't hurt just to discuss the situation. Okay, pick me up around seven." After all, what harm would it do just to consider his proposal?

Blythe walked away from him. Adam ran after her, halting her just as she opened the door. "Who's your doctor?"

"Dr. Meyers. Why do you ask?"

"Thought I'd give him a call and—"

"And see if I'm really pregnant?" She raised her hand against him, wanting nothing more than to slap his face. How dare he think she would humiliate herself this way if she wasn't really pregnant.

Adam grabbed her arm in midair. "To find out what I can do to make this pregnancy easier for you."

"Oh." Blythe jerked her arm away from Adam. "Dr. Meyers, in Decatur. I go back for a checkup in a month."

Adam clasped her chin in his hand. "I'll see you tonight. Until then, take care of yourself and my little girl." He brushed a kiss across her lips.

She stared at him, not returning the kiss, but not fighting the sweet intimacy either. "Tonight," she murmured.

Adam watched Blythe exit the outer office where his secretary sat, staring back and forth from Blythe to him.

"I'm getting married, Sandra. That little redheaded spitfire is my future wife."

"Congratulations, sir. I had no idea you were seriously involved with anyone."

"Oh, I'm as seriously involved with Blythe Elliott as a man can be."

"He asked you to marry him!" Kneeling on the floor in front of her daughter's musical swing, Joy Simpson looked up at Blythe.

"I don't know what I expected." Blythe laid her purse on the work counter in the back room of her florist shop. "But it certainly wasn't a marriage proposal."

Joy wiped the drool from Melissa's rosebud mouth, then stood and wound the swing. A lullaby tinkled sweetly from the music box. Melissa's eyelids drooped.

"Well, I've always considered Adam an honorable man—"

"Ha! If he'd been honorable that night after Missy's christening party, I wouldn't be pregnant right now."

Joy placed her hand on Blythe's shoulder. "It takes two, you know. You were a willing participant in what happened that night."

"Too willing!" Gritting her teeth together, Blythe huffed, then closed her eyes and shook her head. "I can't marry Adam." She rounded the corner of her work counter, removed her purse from the top and slid it onto a bottom shelf.

"I don't think you should make such a hasty decision," Joy said. "After all, you haven't had time to think things through."

"I don't need any time to think about it. I'm not going to marry Adam. We've already made one stupid mistake. It would be ridiculous to make another one."

"Why would marrying Adam be a stupid mistake?"

"How can you ask me that?" Picking up the stack of morning mail and a silver letter opener off her corner desk, Blythe ripped apart the first envelope. "You know how we feel about each other, how we've felt about each other ever since we met. He doesn't approve of the type of woman I am and I certainly don't approve of the type of man he is. In short, Adam Wyatt and I have nothing in common. We'd make each other miserable."

"Well, I will admit you two always did seem to strike sparks off each other. Adam is one of the most old-fashioned guys I know and you're certainly a modern woman. But y'all definitely have something in common now."

"What?"

"A child you created together."

"Oh, that." Blythe sighed. "But I still can't marry him. He's already issuing me orders and we aren't even engaged. I've spent my entire adult life steering clear of entanglements that could lead to marriage and slavery to some chest-beating Neanderthal. You understand why I can't marry Adam, don't you?"

"I understand your reasoning, and I agree that it's usually a mistake to marry someone without love, but you *are* pregnant."

"So?" Shrugging, Blythe opened another envelope, glanced at it and tossed it into the wastebasket. "Single women all across the country are having children alone. There's no reason why I can't do it. After all, I'm a mature woman of twenty-eight, the owner of a fairly successful business and my best friend will be at my side throughout the entire pregnancy. Right?"

"Yes, of course, but what about after the baby's born?" Joy asked. "Craig and I share all the responsibilities of caring for Missy."

"I can take care of a child without a husband."

"Well, don't forget that I'm only working here two days a week now. Who's going to help you take care of the baby when you're at work? You could bring her with you, I suppose, the way I do Missy right now, but doing that every day would be difficult. Could you afford good day care?"

"I'll handle those problems when the time comes. And somehow I'll figure out a solution."

"You're forgetting several important things."

"What things?" Blythe asked.

"Remember where you live and who you are," Joy said. "This isn't New York or L.A. This is Decatur, Alabama. We're living in the heart of the Bible Belt and upstanding citizens who patronize your florist shop don't approve of unwed mothers."

"I know." Frowning, Blythe clicked her teeth and shook her head. "Adam has already pointed out that we have reputations to uphold and an innocent child's future to consider."

"Adam is the other important thing you're forgetting. He's going to want to be a part of the baby's life. Just because you aren't married to him, doesn't eliminate his rights as the child's father."

"Just what are you advising me to do?" Blythe separated the bills from other business correspondence, wrapping a rubber band around each stack.

"Agree to a marriage in name only until after the baby's born. Then get a divorce. Let Adam give the child his name and you two work out child support payments and visitation rights. If you and Adam can learn to get along, it will be the best possible gift the two of you could give your child."

"That's exactly the solution Adam suggested. But maybe we could work things out without getting married. If we get married, he's going to want me to change, and I know I'll want him to change. Each of us will try to make the other become what we want in a mate. Besides, I don't know if it's possible for Adam and me to get along."

Joy smiled. "I think you and Adam have already proved that you can get along. At least for one night."

"Joy!"

"And what's wrong with people changing a little? I know that Adam tends to be a bit old-fashioned, but with some effort on your part, I'll bet you can modernize his thinking."

"I seriously doubt that." Blythe picked up the two stacks of correspondence, handed one to Joy and carried the other toward the small office space at the back of the store.

Flipping through the mail, Joy followed Blythe. "If you've already made up your mind, I don't understand why you agreed to have dinner with him."

"I couldn't think straight after he said he wanted to marry me. He took me off guard. I didn't expect him to take the blame for what happened. It just never occurred to me that he really would want to be involved with the baby."

Shaking her head, Joy sighed. "You really don't know Adam at all, do you? Because he's big, good-looking, very masculine and a real take-charge kind of guy he's always reminded you of your stepfather. You never gave him a chance. Surely the night the two of you made love, you realized that Adam's not like Raymond."

Blythe tossed the stack of bills atop the desk beside the adding machine and computer printer. "I don't think he's *just* like Raymond. I know Adam would never verbally abuse his wife or dominate her so completely that she couldn't think for herself, but—"

"But what?"

"But Adam and I are total opposites. He'd probably expect me to cook dinner every night and do his laundry and things like that. Marriage would be a mistake for us."

"Are you sure?" Joy asked.

"I'm sure. There's no way I'll ever agree to marry Adam."

"Blythe is pregnant, and you're the father?" Craig Simpson's eyes widened, his lips twitched and he coughed a couple of times trying to keep from laughing.

"What the hell's so funny?" Adam paced around his office like a caged tiger. "I got a woman pregnant. And not just any woman, but Blythe Elliott." Rolling his eyes heavenward, Adam shook his head. "The one woman on earth who hates my guts!"

"She must not have hated you the night y'all made love," Craig said.

"I don't know how she felt about me that night." Adam raked his fingers through his thick, silver-streaked black hair. "I've gone over that night a thousand times in my mind. Even before Blythe's revelation today, I've thought about what happened, trying to figure out why we wound up making love. One minute we were arguing, like we always do, then the next minute, a summer storm came up. She'd been crying a lot that day. I wanted to comfort her, and—"

"And the comforting got out of hand?"

"Something like that. It was as if we'd both become two different people, and we wanted each other so much we couldn't keep our hands off each other."

"Opposites attract. Just look at Joy and me."

"Yeah, well, you and Joy were attracted to each other and liked each from the moment y'all met, and you two fell deeply in love. It wasn't that way for Blythe and me." Adam continued pacing back and forth from the wide expanse of windows behind his desk to the closed door that led to his secretary's outer office.

"You and Blythe were attracted to each other from the very beginning, but instead of admitting it, you both fought it. That could be the reason y'all argue every time you're around each other."

"Blythe is not my type. I prefer women who like for a man to be a man. I want a woman who isn't on the defensive all the time. A woman whose career isn't more important to her than her marriage." Adam slumped down in the chair behind his desk. "And I'm not her type, either. I remind her too much of her stepfather, whom she apparently despised."

"So marriage is out of the question, huh?" Leaning his head back against the soft leather of the chair, Craig stretched out his legs in front of him.

"Not necessarily," Adam said. "I think Blythe and I should marry. For the child's sake. And to maintain our respectability. We both have business reputations to consider and we're involved in community affairs. It would be a marriage in name only and we'll divorce after the baby's born. Then we'll share custody."

"Has Blythe agreed to all that?"

"Not yet, but I'm sure she will. After all, it's a good deal for her. I'll give our child my name as well as my love and financial support for the rest of his or her life. And I'll be there throughout the pregnancy to take care of Blythe."

"Blythe isn't the type who'd accept a man's offer to take care of her." Craig laughed. "She's very independent. Joy told me that once Blythe got away from her stepfather and mother, she refused to take anything from them. And Raymond Harold wasn't a poor man. Blythe worked her way through college and has been totally self-supporting since she was eighteen."

"Hey, it's not as if I'm offering to keep her up for the rest of her life. I'll have you draw up the papers. We'll spell everything out in black and white so there won't be any misunderstandings."

"Sounds romantic to me." Craig stared up at the ceiling, missing Adam's menacing glare.

"There's nothing romantic about my relationship with Blythe and you know it. I got her pregnant so I intend to take care of the situation."

"As I recall, you once told me that after what Lynn did to you, you had no desire to ever remarry."

"Yeah, you're right, but I also had no intention of getting a woman pregnant."

"What if Blythe refuses your generous offer?" Craig asked. "She may decide that she can get along just fine without you and your money."

"Oh, she's going to marry me. And she's going to agree to all the conditions. The divorce after the child is born. The generous child support. And joint custody. I'm not going to give her any choice." Adam crossed his arms over his chest.

"It sounds like you don't know Blythe Elliott very well if you think you can bulldoze right over her," Craig said. "She's not the type to take orders, especially from a man."

"I'm not just any man. I'm the father of her baby. I have certain legal rights, don't I?"

"I suggest you don't mention anything about your legal rights to Blythe when you take her out to dinner this evening. Threatening her would be like waving a red flag in front of an angry bull.''

''I have no intention of making any threats as long as Blythe is willing to be reasonable, and I think she will be. After all, it'll be in her best interest to marry me.''

''I'm not sure Blythe will see it that way.''

Leaning over and placing his hands, palms flat, atop his desk, Adam stared at Craig. ''Make no mistake about it, Blythe is going to marry me. Neither of us planned on becoming parents, on having to share a child. I'm sure I'd be at the bottom of her list for possible father candidates, and I can't see Blythe as a mother. She's not nurturing and maternal the way Joy is.''

''Just take my advice, old buddy. Tread lightly where Blythe is concerned. If you push too hard, she'll dig in her heels and fight you to the bitter end.''

''I'll be my most charming self tonight, and I'll make the mother of my unborn child an offer she can't refuse.'' Shoving back his chair, Adam stood, shot out his hand and grinned at Craig. ''You're going to be my best man. Let's shake on it. I'll call you tomorrow and let you know what date Blythe and I decide on tonight.''

# Three

———

**B**lythe knew the minute she took a bite of the orange roughy that she was going to be sick. She'd been foolish to order the fish blackened, but it was one of her favorites. She didn't think she'd ever get used to the idea of this terrible nausea hitting her at odd times of the day and night.

"Excuse me." Shoving her chair away from the table, she stood quickly and made a mad dash through the dimly lit restaurant, only to stop short, realizing she had no idea were the ladies' room was located.

Grabbing a startled waiter by the arm, Blythe felt a sour, burning taste rise in her throat. "Bathroom," she gasped, almost afraid to open her mouth.

"Around the corner, to the right," the wide-eyed young man replied.

Adam caught up with her just as she swung open the door marked Ladies. When he clasped her shoulder in his big hand, she jerked away from him.

"What the devil's the matter?" he asked.

She didn't have time for explanations. If she didn't make it to a sink or commode within a couple of seconds, she would be barfing all over Adam's sleek Italian loafers. She ran inside the rest room, slamming the door in his face.

Adam pounded on the door. "Blythe, are you all right?"

What the hell had happened? They had been eating a delicious meal and actually sharing a pleasant conversation about music. They'd discovered they both shared a love for good jazz. Then all of a sudden, Blythe's face had turned a rather odd shade of greenish white and she'd run from the table as if she were being chased by demons.

"Blythe!"

"May I help you, sir?" a waiter asked.

"Not unless you can find a lady willing to go inside there to see what's wrong with my date."

"Is the young lady sick, sir?"

"I don't know. That's why I need someone to go in there and find out what's going on."

"Well, sir, I'll see what I can do." The waiter walked away.

"Blythe? For the love of Mike, woman, will you answer me!" Adam yelled.

He waited for what seemed like an eternity before an attractive brunette brushed past him and opened the ladies' room door.

"Ma'am." Adam was too worried about Blythe to give a thought to appearing foolish to a stranger.

"Yes." Turning, she smiled, her brown eyes surveying Adam from head to toe.

Any other time he would have been flattered by the woman's blatant appraisal and obvious interest, but right this minute, his only thoughts were of Blythe's well-being.

"My date seems to have taken ill. She's in there, and I have no way of knowing whether or not she needs my help."

The woman laughed. "Oh, I see. Tell me what your date looks like and I'll check on her for you."

"She's a petite redhead. About five-two. And she's wearing a black-and-white halter dress."

"I'll check on her."

"Thanks."

Adam waited a little longer, sweat popping out on his forehead and upper lip. Was it normal for pregnant women to act so strangely? he wondered. Of course, he'd heard about morning sickness, but it wasn't morning now. It was after eight in the evening.

The brown-eyed stranger cracked open the rest room door, peeped out and motioned for Adam.

"Is she all right?" he asked.

"She's been throwing up. She's awfully sick. I took her a damp paper towel, but I swear she looks like she's going to faint any minute now."

Without considering the possible consequences of his actions, Adam shoved the bathroom door completely open and brushed past the brunette. The door to the middle stall stood open. Blythe leaned over the commode, retching.

Grabbing the wet paper towel out of her hand, Adam wiped her face with it. "Morning sickness in the evening? Dammit, Blythe, do you have to do everything backward?"

Gulping for air, she slapped at the arm Adam had draped around her shoulder. "Leave me alone."

"I'm taking you home and we're calling Dr. Meyers."

"I'll be all right. The nausea is better. I don't think I'll throw up again."

"Come on, then." Adam lifted Blythe in his arms. "You scared the devil out of me rushing off the way you did."

"For goodness' sakes, put me down." The words came out in a whisper. Blythe noticed the tall, willowy brunette smiling at them as they passed her on their way out of the ladies' room. "Have you lost your mind!"

Two waiters and the restaurant manager stood in the corridor.

"Is something wrong, Mr. Wyatt?" the manager asked. "How may we be of assistance?"

"Charge dinner to my credit card, and make sure there's a nice tip included," Adam said. "I'm afraid Ms. Elliott is experiencing a little upset stomach. I'm taking her home."

"Oh, dear me. Surely there was nothing wrong with her meal," the manager said.

"Not at all." The manager and both waiters followed Adam through the restaurant and out the front door. "My future wife and I are going to have a baby and she's just suffering a little morning sickness at the wrong time of day."

"Oh!" All three men said in unison.

While waiting for the parking valet to bring around Adam's bright red Lotus, Adam held Blythe in his arms, refusing to put her on her feet despite her squirming and murmured threats.

The fresh air felt wonderful on Blythe's face. She took a deep breath. Dammit, this being pregnant wasn't much fun.

"Why did you do that?" she asked, wishing he'd put her down, infuriated at the idea that they were making spectacles of themselves in public.

"Do what?" he asked innocently.

"Tell the whole world that we're having a baby. Together."

"We are having a baby," he said. "Together."

"I know we are, but you didn't have to announce it to the whole world, did you?"

"Are you ashamed that you're carrying my child?"

"Yes! No! I'm not ashamed of anything. I'm just embarrassed that you proclaimed loud and clear that I'm pregnant, and then carried me out of the restaurant with dozens of people watching. What about our reputations that you were so damn worried about?"

"The fact is you are pregnant, and everyone is going to know in a few months." When the valet parked the car and opened the passenger door, Adam placed Blythe in the seat. "Besides, we didn't want Mr. Dennison to think his delicious food had made you sick, did we? And I did tell them that you were my future wife."

Closing the door, Adam went around and slipped behind the wheel.

"For your information, Adam Wyatt, there is no correct time of day to have morning sickness. It's just a term they use to describe the nausea that can hit a pregnant woman day or night." Blythe slapped at his hands when he double-checked her safety belt. "And I'm not your future wife! I haven't agreed to marry you."

"Will you stop hitting me? I'm getting sick and tired of your slapping me every time I try to help you." Adam started the engine and spun out of the parking lot.

"Then stop trying to be so helpful." Blythe crossed her arms over her chest and sat there sulking. Dinner in Huntsville with Adam had been a mistake. When he'd stopped by her apartment to pick her up, she should have told him then and there that she wasn't going to marry him. If she had, the whole fiasco with dinner never would have happened.

Hell! Adam thought. He'd never known such a disagreeable woman. Didn't she realize that he'd been concerned when she rushed away from the dinner table, that he was still concerned? She was sick because she was pregnant. And he was the man who'd gotten her pregnant.

If only she'd stop resisting him and allow him to help her. Was it going to be like this the whole time she was pregnant, throughout their entire marriage? If so, things weren't going to be easy for either of them. He wasn't used to catering to a woman's whims, and it was more than apparent that Blythe was unaccustomed to a man taking care of her.

Neither of them spoke a word on the ride from the restaurant to Blythe's home on the second floor of a neat, but not so modern, apartment building in southwestern Decatur. By the time Adam got out of the Lotus and made his way around to the passenger door, Blythe had already opened the door and stepped outside onto the sidewalk. She held her house key in her hand.

Oh, yeah, he'd forgotten. She didn't want him opening doors for her, or ordering for her in the restaurant, or doing anything that hinted of old-fashioned good manners.

Blythe gasped suddenly. The night sky swam around and around her. Groaning, she clutched the car door. "Not again."

She hated for Adam to see her like this. Sick and weak. He'd think she was just another helpless female. And that was the last thing Blythe Elliott would ever allow herself to become. Helpless. Her mother had been totally helpless. A weak female who wouldn't fight back when her big, macho husband ordered her around, ridiculed her and turned her into a virtual slave. Blythe couldn't remember her mother ever standing up to her husband. What she did remember, all too well, were the nights she had lain awake for hours listening to her mother's pitiful sobs. She had sworn to herself that no man would ever control her life.

Blythe took a step forward, swayed, then reached out into thin air for support. Adam grabbed her, pulling her up against him.

"Dizzy?" he asked.

"A little," she admitted. "Let's just stand here for a few minutes. I'll be all right."

"You should be inside lying down."

Over her verbal and physical protests, Adam lifted Blythe in his arms and carried her upstairs to her apartment. He jerked the key out of her hand, unlocked the door and carried her inside, feeling for the switch. Finding it, he flipped on the light.

Glancing around the living room, Adam sought out the sofa, a brown-and-tan striped country couch filled with checked, floral and striped throw pillows. A brown-and-coral star quilt hung over one sofa arm.

Adam shoved aside the battered antique oak child's table serving as a coffee table and laid Blythe down on the sofa. When he reached for the quilt, intending to cover her, she glared at him.

"It's September, Adam. I hardly need any cover."

He sat down in the large, brown wicker chair to the right of the sofa. "Can I get you anything? A glass of water? A cola? A shot of whiskey?"

"Plain water will only make me sicker," Blythe said, adjusting a cushion behind her back, already feeling a bit better. "And I don't keep any whiskey in the house. Alcohol isn't good for pregnant women. But I've been drinking sparkling water."

"Is there some in your fridge or do I need to run to the store?"

"There's some in the fridge, but I don't want you waiting on me." Blythe tried to get up, but Adam shoved her gently back down onto the sofa.

"You're doing all the hard work of carrying this baby. I think the least I can do is take care of you a little."

"I don't want anyone taking care of me. I'm a grown woman. I can take care of myself."

Blythe crossed her arms over her chest, a gesture she repeated often and one Adam found more and more irritating.

"I hope you're not going to act like this for the next seven months," Adam said. "If you do, our marriage is going to be unpleasant for both of us."

Adam accidentally ran into the large wooden dollhouse displayed on a low table at the side of the kitchen door. Cursing under his breath, he resisted the urge to kick the table. He opened the kitchen door.

"You don't have to worry about our marriage being unpleasant," Blythe said. "There's not going to be—"

"I can't hear you," Adam called out from the kitchen. "Wait till I come back in there to talk to me."

He had never been in Blythe's kitchen before and the sight that met his eyes came as a surprise. The cabinets had been painted in bright shades of country red, blue and gold. Four mismatched wooden chairs surrounded a small wooden table covered with a wild floral print cloth.

Opening the refrigerator, Adam retrieved a bottle of peach-flavored sparkling water and carried it back into the living room. He unscrewed the lid. Kneeling beside the sofa, he offered the drink to Blythe.

She accepted. "Thanks."

"What were you saying when I was in the kitchen?"

She took several hearty sips of the water. Her stomach growled. She glanced up at Adam. He grinned. She couldn't stop herself from grinning back at him, the action purely involuntary.

"I can't marry you."

He stared at her for several minutes, a strange look on his face, then he stood up and paced around the room.

What did she mean, she couldn't marry him? They hadn't even discussed the plans he'd made. Once she understood that their marriage would be a cut-and-dried business deal, she'd change her mind.

"I'm going to be a part of this pregnancy and a part of my child's life whether or not you and I marry." He stopped pacing, but didn't face Blythe directly. Instead he looked at the warm terra-cotta-colored wall behind the sofa. "Our getting married is for your benefit more than for for mine."

"What do you mean it would be for my benefit?" Blythe sat up straight.

"Well, you'd be a married pregnant lady instead of an unmarried one."

"Big deal." Blythe shrugged. "This is the 1990s, not the 1950s. Unmarried women have babies all the time."

"Not my baby, they don't. And not in Decatur, Alabama."

"Do you want to marry me because you think it's the honorable thing do to?" Blythe asked. And when he didn't respond, only stared at her with an incredulous look, she bristled. "You're a throwback, Mr. Wyatt, to when a man ruled his household with an iron fist, taking care of the little woman because she didn't have sense enough to take care of herself."

Adam balled his hands into fists. "Dammit, Blythe, don't put words in my mouth and don't assume you know the kind of man I am."

"My little girl doesn't need a father who considers her weak and helpless and makes her feel like less than a complete person." Blythe slid her legs off the sofa, her feet touching the floor.

"You have me confused with somebody else." Adam punched his fist into the palm of his other hand, the smacking sound reverberating loudly in the quiet room. "No daughter of mine would ever be weak and helpless, and I would never make her feel less than a complete person. My daughter will know that she's the most special child in the world, and that I'd do anything for her."

"My daughter won't need some man to take care of her!" Blythe jumped up off the sofa, her green-flecked hazel eyes glowering at Adam, daring him to touch her.

"Will you listen to yourself? You aren't thinking rationally. Our child, girl or boy, will need you and me to take care of her or him. Babies need constant care."

Blythe cursed her own stupidity. The flush of anger and embarrassment that crept up her neck and stained her cheeks infuriated her. Of course she knew babies needed constant care. Adam simply didn't understand what she'd meant. Typical man!

"I see no advantage in our getting married." Blythe stood between the sofa and the coffee table, staring Adam straight in the eye. "If I'd known you would try to take charge of my life and my baby, I never would have told you that I was pregnant."

"Well, you did tell me, and I'm glad you did." Adam took a tentative step forward, then stopped when he saw her edging back toward the sofa. "What we both need to do at this point is think about what's best for the baby."

"And just what do you think is best for the baby?"

"Parents who are married when he or she is born. Parents who have worked out an amicable joint custody. A mother who doesn't bad-mouth the father all the time and a father who shows respect for the mother."

In theory, she agreed with Adam, but couldn't help wondering if he really meant what he'd said, or if he was simply adept at telling a woman whatever she wanted to hear. "I see."

"Do you, Blythe? Do you honestly see what I mean?"

Adam made another attempt to approach her. Easing farther away from him, she halted when the back of her legs encountered the sofa. Rounding the edge of the coffee table, he stopped and watched as she toppled down onto the cushions. He sat on the edge of the table, reached out and took her trembling hands into his. She tried to pull out of his grasp. He held tight.

"I don't think we can live together. We'd never get along, and our bickering constantly would be bad for the baby." Blythe tugged on her hands. "Please let me go."

Adam ran his thumbs up and down the sides of Blythe's hands. She sucked in her breath. He felt a tightening in himself, from his chest to his knees.

"We'll have a marriage in name only," Adam said. "I'll go to Lamaze classes with you and see you through the birthing process. And after the baby is born and you've recuperated, we'll get a divorce. I'll support my daughter or my son financially. I'll even build you and the child a house."

"That's all very generous of you. What do you get out of it?"

"I get to experience every aspect of fatherhood."

"And?"

"I'll want joint custody."

"Exactly what do you mean by joint custody?" she asked.

"The child spends part of the time with you and part of the time with me. We can work out the details any way we think is best for the child."

Blythe looked down at her hands. Adam released them.

"I don't want to marry you, and if you're honest with yourself, you don't want to marry me. Despite the fact that we slept together, we don't really like each other."

"Maybe we could learn to like each other." Adam stood, pushing the table back with his legs. "If we gave each other half a chance and really got to know each other, we might learn to be friends."

"I doubt that will ever happen."

"Why not?" Adam grinned. "A few months ago neither of us would have believed we'd ever become lovers, and look what happened."

Blythe groaned. "The best I can promise is that I'll think about it. I'll consider everything you've said."

"How long will you need to think about it?"

"How long?"

"Yes, how long?" he asked. "We don't have all the time in the world, you know. I don't want us saying I do when they wheel you into the delivery room."

"I won't allow you to boss me around or make my decisions for me. And I won't sleep with you."

"If I agree to those stipulations, will you marry me?"

"I don't know. I have to think about it."

"I'll give you until Saturday night. I'll pick you up for dinner and we'll make wedding plans." Adam walked across the room, opened the front door and turned around, looking back at Blythe. "I have a couple of stipulations when we get married, too. You won't try to exclude me from anything that concerns our child, and you won't see any other men for the duration of our marriage."

Blythe's mouth fell open. "You don't want me to see other men?" She laughed, shaking her head in disbelief. "In a few months I'm going to look like a Volkswagen Beetle and you're afraid I'll be painting the town red with other men."

"My first wife made a fool of me." Adam took a deep breath. "Even if our marriage isn't going to be a real one, I don't relish being made a fool of again."

"What about you? Would you... I mean, since we won't be having sex, would you go to another woman?"

"I think I can manage celibacy for the next seven or eight months," Adam said, hating the very thought and hoping Blythe wouldn't make them adhere to that particular rule.

"Then we both agree to no other sexual partners during the duration of our marriage, right?"

Adam tried not to grin. Did she realize exactly how she'd phrased her question? No other sexual partners didn't exclude them from having sex with each other.

"I promise," he said. "No other sexual partners."

"All right," Blythe agreed. "I'll consider your proposal, but I don't promise you an answer by Saturday night."

Adam closed the door, walked to his car, got in and drove away, whistling all the while.

*His arms surrounded her as she laid her head on his shoulder. She felt the heat in him, the strength and masculine power. Relaxing against him, she whispered his name.*

*"Adam."*

*Cocooned in the warmth of his embrace, Blythe found herself longing for more—wanting and needing to take this big, gentle man into her body. To know once again the sheer joy of his possession.*

*When his lips covered hers, she sighed with pleasure, lifting her arms to circle his neck.*

*"Sweet, lovely Blythe." He traced the planes of her face with his fingertips, allowing his hand to travel downward, over her neck and collarbone, easing the sheet away from her naked breasts.*

*She cried out when he caressed her. "Please, Adam."*

*"Slower this time, babe," he said. "We'll make it last all night."*

The jarring ring of Blythe's alarm clock intruded on her dream, rousing her from the hazy sweetness of a moment that had seemed so real.

She slapped the clock, shutting off the alarm. With her eyes still closed, she threw back the covers and stretched.

She didn't want to awaken and face the reality of another day. She wanted to stay in her dream, in that safe, secure place where no one existed except Adam and her.

Blythe's eyes flew open. She jerked straight up in bed. What was she thinking? Had she lost her mind? Again? She'd been reliving that night at Adam's condo. The night they had made love. The night she'd gotten pregnant.

Jumping out of bed, she slipped her feet into her pink leather house shoes and headed straight for the bathroom. What she needed was a shower and strong cup of coffee to clear her head and erase any foolish notions about Adam Wyatt.

Then she remembered. No caffeine. Doctor's orders. Well, maybe she could pretend the decaf she'd been drinking would work as well as regular coffee. Being pregnant certainly had its drawbacks. In her case, Adam Wyatt was one of the biggest drawbacks.

Turning on the shower, Blythe stripped out of her pink teddy, picked up a washcloth off the small stack she'd placed on the back of the commode, and stepped beneath the warm water.

These dreams had to stop! she told herself. Ever since that night—the night she'd gone completely mad—she'd been dreaming about Adam Wyatt making love to her. And as if it weren't bad enough that she dreamed about him, she'd catch herself, at odd times during the day, thinking about him, remembering the things he'd said. Remembering the way he'd touched her, and the way she'd touched him.

For the life of her, she couldn't understand what had happened to her that night. One minute she and Adam had been arguing, as usual, and then the next minute they were making love. And she'd wanted him. Wanted him more than she'd ever wanted anything in her life. Instead of making her wary and defensive the way other men often did, indeed the way he normally did, Adam had made her feel completely safe and secure in the heat of their passion.

For all his strength, he had been a tender, caring lover. Even the first time, when they'd practically ripped off each other's clothes, his wild passion had been tempered with a sort of savage gentleness.

That night she had come to know a different Adam. Now she wondered if that man even existed, except in her imagination.

Blythe lathered her body with the jasmine-scented soap she'd used for years. When her hand touched her breasts, she sighed, unable to stop herself from remembering the feel of Adam's hands on her body, the delicious torment of his mouth. No, the Adam who had made love to her wasn't imaginary. He'd been real—as real as the man who wanted to marry her and be a father to their child.

Rivulets of steamy water cascaded down Blythe's petite body. She laid her hand over her flat stomach. Adam was right. They had to do what was best for the baby. She just wasn't sure marrying Adam was the best thing to do.

The lines of print on Adam's morning paper ran together, a blurry mix of black and white. Closing his eyes, he rubbed them with his thumb and index finger, pinching the bridge of his nose.

He had to stop thinking about Blythe! The woman was driving him crazy. Ever since the night they'd made love, she'd been creeping into his thoughts, taunting him with the memories of those passionate hours they'd spent in his bed. After over two months of trying to figure out exactly what had happened and why, Adam was no closer to discovering the truth than he'd been the morning after. He and Blythe didn't like each other, had never liked each other. From the moment they'd met, Blythe had been defensive and hostile. Although he occasionally found her smart mouth and I-am-woman attitude amusing, Adam usually considered Blythe Elliott a royal pain in the butt.

And if anyone had ever asked him, he would have told them that, despite finding Blythe extremely attractive, he'd never risk having a relationship with her. So, what had happened that night? He had looked into those beautiful hazel eyes and been lost. In those few brief minutes before they'd both lost control, he'd seen a side of Blythe he'd never known existed. The soft, feminine side of her, the side of her that wanted and needed a man. And he had wanted to be that man more than he'd ever wanted anything in his life.

If only he'd used protection the first time they made love, as he did the other two times, then they wouldn't be faced with the dilemma of Blythe's pregnancy. He blamed himself, not her. Even though he'd had no idea she was still a virgin, the fault had been his. Not once, since his divorce, had he had unprotected sex. Not until Blythe Elliott had wrapped her arms around him and driven him insane. Insane with desire.

Adam laughed. Who would have believed that little Miss Blythe, with her cropped-off cinnamon hair, her freckled nose, her sassy mouth and air of independence would have laid him low? He'd known his share of women, but no one quite like Blythe.

For the life of him, he couldn't picture Blythe as a mother. She was a fidgety little ball of fire. He didn't see anything maternal about her. But like it or not, she was going to have his baby, and it was up to him to make sure she became the best mother possible.

He hadn't thought much about fatherhood, not since the days when he and Lynn had tried to have a child. He hadn't planned to ever remarry. The first experience had been far too painful. He'd loved Lynn, had set her on a pedestal, had given her everything her heart desired. And she had betrayed him with another man. After eight years, the pain was gone, but the bitterness remained. Sometimes he wondered if it would ever go away.

Maybe he and Blythe were well suited, after all. He didn't trust women and she didn't trust men. But how would they ever get beyond the distrust and become the kind of parents their child deserved?

The first order of business, after Blythe became his wife, was for them to learn how to be friends. Once they divorced and shared custody of their child, they would need to be able to present a united front, to make decisions jointly.

He was willing to do whatever was necessary for the sake of the baby. The child was what mattered. His child.

His and Blythe's.

# Four

Blythe had taken her own sweet time making a decision about marrying Adam. She hadn't allowed him to bully her, despite his constant harassment. The way he'd ranted and raved, pleaded and coaxed, you'd have thought he wanted to marry her more than anything else in the world. Blythe knew better. Adam Wyatt, old-fashioned macho jerk that he was, thought he was doing the honorable thing. He didn't any more want to be married to her than she did to him.

But there was a child involved. And in the end, the baby they shared seemed far more important than what either Adam or she wanted.

Today was her wedding day. She was three months pregnant and already beginning to show just a little. Although no one else would notice the change in her body, she was all too aware of it. Her once flat stomach protruded just the tiniest bit. Her breasts had filled out some, and her face appeared slightly rounder.

Adam had offered to pay for whatever kind of wedding she wanted. White gown and a dozen bridesmaids, he'd told her, if that would make her happy. The offer had been tempting, the realization of every little girl's fantasy wedding, but she had declined. After all, theirs wouldn't be a real marriage, so this wouldn't be a real wedding, just a legal procedure to make their child legitimate and thus protect the child and themselves from being socially ostracized.

Adam had offered her a honeymoon, a trip anywhere in the world she wanted to go. She'd declined that offer, too. Honeymoons were for lovers, which she and Adam would never be again.

Ultimately, they had agreed on a small, very private ceremony at Joy's father's home in the Delano Park area of Decatur, with Joy and Craig standing up with them. Blythe had no family, since her mother's death in an airplane crash six years ago. And she hadn't felt comfortable inviting any of her other friends and acquaintances, women who would never understand how she'd gotten herself into such a predicament.

Adam had promised not to invite any friends or business associates if she would agree to a reception honoring their marriage sometime in the next few weeks. Reluctantly, Blythe had accepted Adam's deal, dreading the thought of being put on display and wondering how many people would guess the reason she and Adam had married.

"Are you ready?" Joy asked, holding out Blythe's bridal bouquet of pale pink roses.

Forcing a smile, Blythe accepted the flowers. "I don't think I'll ever be ready to marry Adam, but we've made our bargain and signed all the legal documents. The only thing left to do is make it official."

"You know, marrying the father of your child isn't the worst thing that could happen to you."

"It is when the man is Adam Wyatt."

Joy patted Blythe on the back. "Poor Blythe, being forced to marry a wealthy, handsome man who just happens to be one of the nicest guys I've ever known. He's considered the best catch in the entire state of Alabama."

"Lucky me." Blythe squared her shoulders, took a deep breath and glanced at the closed bedroom door. "Your opinion of Adam greatly differs from mine."

"That's because my opinion of men in general greatly differs from yours. If you expect the worst from a man, then you'll never trust him. You'll always be waiting for him to make a mistake. If you and Adam have any hope of cementing some kind of bond for the sake of your child, then y'all are going to have to learn to trust each other."

"His wife hurt him terribly, didn't she?" Blythe asked.

"Craig says that when he first became Adam's lawyer, about a year after the divorce, he'd never seen a guy in so much pain." Joy straightened the collar on Blythe's pale pink silk suit. "For a couple of years after the divorce, he drank too much, had too many one-night stands and pretty much became impossible to be around."

While the tears gathered in the corners of her eyes, Blythe laughed. "Please tell me that I'm not making the second biggest mistake of my life."

"You're not making a mistake," Joy assured her. "Marrying Adam is probably the smartest thing you've ever done. By the time your baby is born, I have a feeling that the whole experience will have made you and Adam better people."

Music drifted upward from the parlor downstairs. Blythe had asked Joy to choose something appropriate, but definitely not the wedding march. She'd had no idea that Joy would hire a harpist and violinist. The music was far too romantic for a shotgun wedding.

Joy opened the door that led out into the upstairs hallway. "Ready?"

"No, but let's go ahead and get this over with."

Joy, dressed in a lavender silk suit similar to Blythe's and carrying a small bouquet of violets, preceded Blythe down the staircase, across the foyer and into the front parlor of Franklin Daniels's Victorian home.

Craig stood beside Adam, both men in black suits, a pink rosebud boutonniere in Adam's lapel. Blythe held her head high as she entered the parlor, her gaze focused on the open Bible the minister held in his hands.

The harpist and violinist created the sweet, pure strands of "Ave Maria." Tears lodged in Blythe's throat and shimmered in her eyes. When she handed Joy her bouquet, Adam reached out and took Blythe's hand in his. His flesh was warm, his grip gentle yet strong. Her hand trembled.

Adam brought her hand to his lips, kissing her tenderly. She glanced up at him. He smiled, then lowered his head and whispered in her ear. "Everything will be all right. I promise."

Nodding her head, Blythe squeezed Adam's hand, and together they turned to face the minister.

Afterward, she could remember very little of the ceremony. Undoubtedly she'd said and done all the appropriate things because she heard the minister proclaim them man and wife. A wide gold band glistened on the third finger of her left hand; its mate circled Adam's finger.

What she would never forget was Adam kissing her. Since he'd had to lift her off her feet, she'd instinctively grabbed him for support, surprised by his action. She had expected a quick, pleasant kiss, if anything. Instead she'd received and returned a long, tender yet disturbingly passionate kiss.

When Joy paraded Blythe and Adam into her father's elegant dining room, Blythe gasped at the sight of the wedding cake, three and a half feet high, decorated with cream frosting and pink baby roses.

"Joy, what have you done?" Blythe asked.

"Just a little wedding cake and some champagne. Except the bride gets ginger ale."

Joy smiled so happily that Blythe didn't have the heart to chastise her friend. She couldn't tell her that by trying to turn the event into something romantic, she was making the whole affair twice as difficult for Blythe.

"Have you got the camera, Daddy?" Joy motioned for her short, squat father to take some pictures, then she turned to Blythe and Adam. "Come on, you two, cut the cake."

Joy ushered them over to the table. All the while Adam kept his arm around Blythe's waist.

"After you cut it, Blythe, you feed Adam a piece and then he feeds you a piece," Joy said. "Get some pictures of this, Daddy."

Franklin complied, although he grumbled about Joy not hiring a professional photographer. Joy hushed him, whispering that Blythe had forbidden her to hire one.

"Come on, babe." Adam lifted the silver knife, offering it to his bride. He covered her hand with his. "Don't spoil this for Joy. She's gone to a lot of trouble to make this day special for us."

"I know." Blythe smiled for the camera.

With his hands over hers, Adam and Blythe cut the cake, and obedient to Joy's orders, took turns feeding each other pieces.

"Do you two have honeymoon plans?" Franklin asked.

"Not exactly," Adam said.

"Not at all," Blythe said.

"Well, that won't do." Franklin took another picture, one of the bride frowning at the groom.

"I explained the situation to you, Daddy." Joy laid her hand on her father's back. "Adam and Blythe aren't having a honeymoon. They're just going home and starting their life together."

Blythe shivered, the thought of starting a life with Adam quite intimidating, the idea of living with him almost frightening. How would they handle the intimate day-to-day living arrangements? She hadn't wanted to leave her home. It had taken her years to decorate the three-room apartment just the way she wanted it. Adam had asked her to move into his condo, but she hated the sleek, modern, glass-and-chrome masculinity of his place. And she knew staying in his home would constantly remind them both of the night they'd spent in his king-size bed.

When she had suggested that they not live together, Adam had adamantly rejected the proposal. He'd told her, in no uncertain terms, that he didn't intend to miss one minute of her pregnancy from here on out.

So, they had compromised. Temporarily, at least. They would move into the house that had once belonged to Adam's father, a neat little cottage on the outskirts of Decatur, not far from Mallard Creek and only a few miles from Joy and Craig's home in a new, exclusive subdivision. The house had three bedrooms, so they could have their privacy, and although Adam would have a long drive into his Huntsville office, Blythe would be fairly close to Petals Plus in Decatur.

Her job had created another disagreement over terms. Adam had insisted there was no reason for her to work while she was pregnant. She had reminded him that she wasn't simply an employee at Petals Plus, but the owner. They had agreed to disagree on several points, but in the end, they had again compromised. Blythe would hire a couple of part-time employees to help her on the days Joy didn't work.

Glancing around the room, Adam noticed the way Joy and Craig and Mr. Daniels were looking at Blythe and him. "I think they're expecting us to dance." He grasped her by the arm.

"What?" She stared at him, dazed by the day's events, her mind still a bit foggy with thoughts of what the future would bring.

Adam pulled Blythe into his arms. "One dance to please Joy, and then I think we can slip away."

Blythe allowed him to lead her into a slow dance, his strong arms holding her close. She shivered. Every time she got near Adam, her body remembered the night of passion they had shared and reacted with a trembling desire she could not deny.

They moved slowly to the romantic tune, Adam smiling at her as if he were happy, as if he hadn't just married a woman who didn't want to be his wife.

Adam knew that the wedding had been more difficult for Blythe than for him, even though the whole affair had been just one step above a root canal for him. If Blythe wasn't so damned and determined not to like him, to keep him at arm's length for the duration of their marriage, then he might be able to find the situation tolerable. As things stood, he now faced seven months, plus whatever time it took to get a divorce, of celibacy as well as a marriage of convenience to a woman who was bound to make his life hell.

But a man did what a man had to do. And that meant marrying the woman who was carrying his child.

Even if it killed him in the process, he planned to take care of Blythe, to make the next seven months as easy for her as he possibly could.

He just hoped she'd meet him halfway.


Blythe and Adam stood on the front porch of his father's cottage. His dad had once told Adam he'd proudly purchased it for Adam's mother a few years after their marriage. Adam unlocked the door, then turned around and lifted Blythe into his arms.

"What are you doing?" Narrowing her eyes, she puckered her mouth into a frown.

"Carrying the bride across the threshold," he said, walking into the living room.

"You're being ridiculous," she told him. "You've let that silly wedding Joy gave us go to your head. Put me down!"

Adam lowered Blythe to her feet ever so slowly, allowing her to slide sensuously down his big body. Gasping, she jumped away from him.

He turned on the lights, revealing the tan-and-blue living room and adjoining dining area. The table held a bouquet of pink roses and a bottle of chilled sparkling apple juice.

"I suppose Joy did that, too." Blythe glanced around at the large airy rooms, the clear, sharp coolness of the colors and the light oak furniture. Obviously, the home had been decorated to suit a man's tastes.

"The roses and the sparkling apple juice?" Adam asked.

"No, they were my idea."

"Oh."

"I had your things put in the largest bedroom, the one on the left, with a bath to itself." Adam took off his coat, removed his tie and unbuttoned his shirt, then tossed the coat and tie on the back of the sofa.

"Thank you. I think I'll go change out of this suit and into some jeans." Blythe had to get away from Adam, away from those dark eyes that seemed to be asking her questions she didn't want to answer.

She opened the bedroom door and flipped on the wall switch. She gasped. What had happened to this room? She well remembered it from when Craig and Joy had lived here over a year ago, while their new home was under construction just down the road. This room had been decorated in brown and green, the furniture and accessories totally masculine.

Maybe she had misunderstood Adam and gone into the wrong room. No. Her clothes hung in the open closet, and her toiletries lined the top of the dressing table.

The room had been freshly painted a pale pink—her favorite color. The furniture was mahogany, each piece an antique. A pink-and-multipastel-colored quilt adorned the canopy bed. Lace pillows completely covered the headboard.

Blythe bit her bottom lip. Tears gathered in the corners of her eyes. Damn him! Damn Adam Wyatt! Why had he gone and done something so totally romantic, so sweet and caring? He'd had the room completely redecorated—for her.

Brushing the tears from her eyes, she rummaged in the closet until she found a pair of old faded jeans and a short-sleeved, red cotton-knit sweater. She kicked her heels off, slipped out of her panty hose and sighed.

Just as she wiggled into her jeans, finding they wouldn't button due to the slight increase in her waistline, Blythe heard music coming from the living room. A cool jazz rendition of "Summertime." Goose bumps covered her flesh.

She couldn't let things get to her—her romantic wedding, Adam carrying her across the threshold, this beautiful pink bedroom. No, Blythe would not allow anything to make her weak and vulnerable. Letting down her defenses was what had gotten her into this mess in the first place. Adam Wyatt's reputation with women was no secret. He knew exactly all the right buttons to push to seduce a woman into doing whatever he wanted her to do.

Sucking in her breath, Blythe tried again to fasten her jeans, but they just wouldn't meet. Adam chose that precise moment to knock on the door and walk in. Glancing at her unbuttoned jeans, he grinned.

"Looks like we'll have to get you some maternity clothes pretty soon," he said.

"No, we won't." Blythe jerked down her sweater to cover her waist. "These jeans were always a bit snug."

"They're very becoming. I like the way they fit you."

Placing her hands on her hips, she glared at him. "Did you want something? Was there a reason you came barging in here, uninvited?"

Did he want something? Yeah, he wanted a wedding night. Was there a reason he'd come to her room? Yeah, foolishly, he'd thought she might thank him for having everything completely redone, just for her.

"Uninvited?" Adam asked. "Do I need an invitation to come into your bedroom?"

"You certainly do and you know it. If we're going to live together, then you'll have to learn to respect my privacy."

Adam huffed, letting out a deep breath. Hell, so it was starting already! How was he going to live through seven months of this? Marriage to a shrew hadn't been one of his lifelong dreams.

"I won't come in here again without an invitation," Adam said. "I just came this time to tell you that I'd poured us some sparkling apple juice and put on a CD. I thought you might want to come out to the living room and sit and talk awhile."

Blythe wished she hadn't overreacted. What had she thought he wanted? To ravish her? To sweep her off her feet and carry her to his bed, against her will? "Talk about what?"

"Just talk." Adam shrugged. "We could set up some house rules, things like my not coming into your bedroom uninvited."

"All right. I suppose we do need to decide on the best way to keep from annoying each other."

Barefoot, Blythe followed Adam out to the living room and sat down on the big, overstuffed sofa. He handed her a champagne flute of sparkling apple juice, then lifted his own glass.

"How about a toast?"

Blythe nodded agreement.

"Here's to tolerating each other for seven months and trying our best to become friends for the sake of our child."

Blythe sipped the drink. Was there any hope for Adam and her? Could they become friends? Was it possible? "I'm sorry I snapped your head off about coming into my room. It's just that I don't want—"

"There's no reason for you to be afraid of me, Blythe. I don't have any sinister plan to seduce you, if that's what's worrying you." Adam finished off the sparkling juice quickly and set the glass down on the coffee table. "What happened between us the night after Melissa's christening party is as much a mystery to me as it is to you."

She willed herself not to blush. Damn her redhead's complexion. "You know this isn't what I wanted. I mean, you and me stuck with each other like this."

"I know, and I'm sorry," he said.

"So am I, but I guess it's too late for either of us to be sorry." Blythe tucked her feet up on the sofa. "After Joy got pregnant with Melissa, I realized how much I wanted a child of my own. I wasn't planning on getting married, so I assumed I would never get pregnant. Boy, was I wrong." Blythe tried to laugh, but the sound came out a mixture of gasp and sigh.

"We're not the first two people to get caught in the tender trap, and we won't be the last." Adam sat down beside Blythe, resting one arm across the back of the sofa.

"The tender trap," Blythe repeated the phrase. "That's what we are, aren't we, Adam? Trapped. Trapped by our own stupidity."

"Trapped by our desire." His voice was deep and low. He stole a glance at Blythe, who stared at him, her eyes filled with tears.

"We must never let our child know that we felt trapped because of her," Blythe said. "She must always feel loved and wanted, no matter what."

"Don't worry. I want only what's best for our child," Adam assured her. "That's what this marriage is all about, isn't it? Doing what's best for the baby."

"Yes, that's what this marriage is all about." Blythe smiled. "So, if we're going to be living together for the next few months, we might as well go ahead and set up some rules. Right? We've taken care of all the legalities, so we might as well get down to deciding how we're going to live from day to day."

"There's no need for you to try to handle the house-cleaning with a full-time job," Adam said. "I can bring Pearl in to take care of things."

"Someone to do the cleaning isn't necessary. I've never had a maid and I don't want one. We can take care of things ourselves, don't you think? Or do you believe housecleaning is women's work?''

"I think I'd prefer having Pearl come in and do the work, but if you don't want her, we'll compromise and I'll bring her in once a week, to do the heavy stuff. Temporarily.''

Blythe gave him a cold, disapproving look. "All right, but what about the cooking?'' she asked. "I think you and I should take turns, if that's okay with you.''

"I'm not much of a cook," Adam said. "I thought you'd take care of that. I assume you know how to cook, don't you?''

"Yes, I know how to cook.'' And before we end this marriage, buddy boy, you'll know how to cook, too, Blythe thought.

"Good, I'm looking forward to a home-cooked meal every night,'' Adam said.

Blythe smiled, the gesture a phony pose. It was starting already, just as she knew it would. He wanted the little woman to have his dinner waiting for him when he came home from work.

"I'll gladly put dinner on the table every other night,'' Blythe told him. "On the other nights, it will be your responsibility. And don't worry, you don't have to cook, unless you want to. Takeout will be fine with me.''

Adam grimaced, but nodded agreement. "All right. Fine. We'll compromise on meal preparations.''

Blythe wanted to get a few other things straight while they were discussing house rules. No matter what Adam had said, she thought he probably planned on sharing her bed every night. Well, he had another think coming!

"I won't enter your room uninvited and you won't come into mine,'' she said.

"Agreed.''

"I usually go in to work around nine, so I get up at seven. We could have breakfast together, if you want.'' Blythe couldn't imagine what it would be like to sit across the breakfast table from Adam Wyatt every morning. "Of course, some mornings I can't eat anything."

"You mean you actually get morning sickness in the morning?" He chuckled.

She laughed, too. "Dr. Meyers said it shouldn't last much longer."

"I want to go with you for your next checkup."

"That won't be for a another few weeks."

"I want to make sure I do everything possible to help you have a good pregnancy." Adam would do anything and everything he could to keep Blythe safe and well and make sure nothing happened to their child. Despite the circumstances of the child's conception, Adam wanted this baby. He'd never realized how much he wanted a child until that day, over a month ago, when Blythe had walked into his office and announced she was pregnant.

"I intend to go through natural child birth." Blythe watched Adam closely for a reaction, but he just looked at her as if waiting for her to continue. "If you would rather not be my coach, then I'll ask Joy. I know she'd be more than happy to—"

"You won't need to ask Joy. We're going to do this together, remember?"

Crisscrossing her arms over her chest, Blythe hugged her shoulders. Did she want Adam to share everything with her? She wasn't sure. If he really was her husband, and not just in name only, it would be different. If their child had been conceived in love and not in passion. She could barely think of the word where she and Adam were concerned, but she would be lying to herself if she pretended that their one night together hadn't been filled with passion. But love? No, there was no love.

Was a man like Adam Wyatt even capable of love? He was quite capable of passion and possessiveness and even protectiveness, but love? She seriously doubted it.

And what about her? She loved Joy and Melissa and truly cared for Craig. She had once loved her mother, loved her long after she had ceased to respect her. But love a man? Perhaps she was as incapable of love as Adam appeared to be.

But even if she and Adam could never love each other, they could love their child. Blythe laid her hand over her stomach. She already loved her baby. Her little girl.

Adam watched Blythe closely, noting the way she covered her slightly round tummy with her hand. What was she thinking? he wondered. Did she wish she wasn't pregnant? Was she regretting her decision to have the baby? Once their child was born, would Blythe become the kind of mother his own mother had been and decide her freedom was far more important than a child? If that did happen, he would be there for his son or daughter, the way his father had been there for him.

"I suppose there are things we'll just have to learn as we go along." Blythe slid her feet off the sofa. "I've never lived with a man. I mean—"

"It's all right," Adam said. "Even though we're living in the same house doesn't mean we're really *living* together. You don't have to keep reminding me that there's not going to be any hanky-panky."

"You're right. I'm sorry." Blythe stood. "I think I'll say good-night. This has been a long day and I'm tired."

"I'll see you in the morning."

Adam watched her walk down the hall and into her room. Her room. The room that he'd always used when he stayed at the cottage. The room he'd hired an interior designer to completely make over just for Blythe, following Joy's suggestions.

Adam went into the guest room, the one that had been his own room when he'd lived at home, years ago. His father had remained in the house until his sudden death of a heart attack twelve years ago. Adam had never brought a woman to his father's home, but now he'd be living here with his wife.

*His wife!*

Adam stripped, flung his clothes on the floor, dug his silk robe out of his suitcase and went into the bathroom shared by the other small bedroom. Turning on the shower, he stepped inside, threw back his head and let the warm water caress his body.

Drying off quickly, he rubbed the dampness from his hair and decided to wait until morning to shave. It wasn't as if anyone would complain about the dark stubble covering his jaw. Blythe sure as hell wasn't going to get close enough to even notice, let alone be irritated by the feel.

Adam switched off the lights in his bedroom and climbed into bed. Minutes ticked by, turning into an hour, then two. Adam tossed and tumbled. Dammit, why couldn't he sleep? Just because this was his wedding night was no reason to torment himself. Knowing his wife was only a few yards away, across the hall, drove him crazy wondering what it would be like to make love to her again. Could it possibly be as good as it had been that first and only night they'd shared?

She didn't want him. She'd made that perfectly clear. So what the hell was wrong with him? Why did he want a woman who didn't want him, a woman he wasn't sure he even liked?

Finally Adam dozed off, a restless, on-and-off slumber, punctuated with fragmented dreams. Dreams of Blythe lying naked in his arms, whimpering, begging him to make love to her, crying out his name in fulfillment.

Adam woke with a start, sweat coating his naked chest and arms. He needed a drink. Something to help him sleep.

He put on his silk robe and quietly opened his bedroom door. When he stepped out into the hall, he heard a peculiar sound. Sobbing. Hushed, choking sobs. Blythe? Blythe was crying.

He reached out, grabbing the brass knob of her bedroom door. Then he remembered she had told him never to enter her bedroom without an invitation. He leaned against the door, listening, hearing his own thundering heartbeat and the soft, muffled sobs coming from the other side of the closed door.

Adam knocked softly. No response. The crying stopped. He knocked again, a little harder.

"Yes?" Blythe sounded like a little girl, her voice whispery and childlike.

"May I come in?"

"No, I... What do you want, Adam?"

"I heard you crying. I just want to make sure you're all right."

"I'm all right!" Her voice, though shaky, was much stronger.

"How do I know you are?"

"Oh, all right, then, come in and see for yourself."

Adam eased open the door. Blythe sat in the middle of the bed, holding the sheet up to her chin. The room was bathed in moonlight that filtered through the white lace curtains at the windows.

Adam walked over to the bed, turned on the nightstand lamp and looked down at Blythe. Her hair was tousled, her eyes swollen, her nose red. Dear God, how long had she been crying?

"You're not all right. What is it, babe? What's wrong?" He wanted to reach out and touch her, to put his arms around her and comfort her. He didn't dare.

"How can you ask me what's wrong?" She held on to the sheet as if those few yards of pink satin were the only thing keeping her safe. "I—I'm pregnant and married to you." She gulped down a sob. "And stop calling me babe!"

Adam shrugged. "You sound as if that's a fate worse than death."

He sat on the bed beside her. She edged slowly away from him, inch by inch, until her back was against the headboard.

"I know I should be grateful. Joy as much as told me so. You were considered the best catch in the state of Alabama. Did you know that? And I caught you." Tears filled

Blythe's eyes. "I caught you in the tender trap. That is what you called it, isn't it? Well, it doesn't feel very much like a tender trap to me, does it to you? It feels like a steel trap crushing the life out of me."

"I'm sorry you feel that way." What the hell was he supposed to say or do? His wife had been sitting there for hours bawling her eyes out because she was married to him.

"It's not your fault," she said.

"Then whose fault is it?" he asked.

"Okay, so it is your fault. And my fault, too. This is my wedding night and all I can think about is—" Good grief, she'd been about to say that all she could think about was the night they'd spent together making love.

"All you can think about is what, Blythe?"

"Is that a wedding night shouldn't be like this."

"What should a wedding night be like?"

Tears created two damp trails down her cheeks. She loosened her hold on the sheet in order to wipe her face with her fingertips. Adam sucked in his breath when he saw the hot pink teddy she wore. Damn, redheads weren't supposed to look good in pink. Blythe did. Right now, she looked good enough to eat.

Blythe sobbed harder and harder. "Happy.... Wedding nights...should—" Sob. Sob. Sob. "—be happy."

"You're right, a wedding night should be happy." To hell with not touching her! Adam pulled Blythe into his arms. She went without a fight, her body stiff as a board. "What can I do to make you happy?"

She stared at him, her vision blurred with tears, her body quivering. "I'm not going to have sex with you. No sex. That was part of our bargain."

"Okay, sex is out. So what else could I do to make you happy?" Adam grinned.

Pulling away, she glared at him, then hit him on the arm as hard as she could. "This isn't funny."

"Ouch!" Adam grabbed her and kissed her on the nose. "You don't think this situation is funny? Well, I do. Here we are, married less than twenty-four hours and all we've done is argue, except when you've been crying. I offer to make you happy by having sex with you and you turn me down without telling me what else I could do for you."

"You can't do anything for me, but leave me alone."

"Well, I can't just walk out of here and let you cry the rest of the night."

"Why should you care?"

"Your being so upset isn't good for the baby." He'd said the first thing that had come to his mind, an explanation he thought Blythe would accept without an argument.

"Oh." He was right of course. But she felt even more like crying now that he'd reminded her—reminded her that the only thing that mattered to him was the baby.

"So, what can I do to make you and our baby happy tonight?"

"You could pop us some popcorn, open us some more of that sparkling apple juice, and sit up the rest of the night with me watching the Dracula marathon they're showing on TV this weekend." What on earth had made her suggest something so idiotic to Adam? He'd think she was crazy. It didn't matter that if she had been home alone this Saturday night, that's exactly what she would be doing.

"You like old horror movies?" Adam asked.

"I love them."

"Me, too."

"You're kidding?"

"Come on, babe, I'm fixing to make you a happy woman." Standing, Adam offered her his hand.

"Give me my robe." She pointed to the foot of the bed. "And don't call me babe."

He tossed her the hot pink-lavender-and-teal floral robe. Blythe slipped into it, tied the belt and jumped out of bed.

When the first pale glow of dawn spread across the sky, Blythe lay in Adam's arms on the living room sofa. She slept peacefully, cuddled close to his warmth. A bowl of popcorn kernels rested on the coffee table, along with two empty glasses. Black-and-white images flickered across the television screen as Dracula seduced a beautiful young victim.

Adam stroked Blythe's arm. She was so tiny, so fragile. And the most exasperating female he'd ever known. But there was something vulnerable about Blythe Elliott. No, not Blythe Elliott. Blythe Wyatt. And there was a lot more to his new bride than met the eye. Beneath her defiant, independent-woman facade, beat the heart of a lonely, unhappy little girl.

If he could be patient and gentle and kind, would she allow him to take care of her? Would she ever learn to trust him? Or would the next seven months be a constant struggle of wills?

What did he expect from Blythe? From himself? From their marriage? Sitting there, holding her, his body hard with desire, Adam cursed himself for a fool. He had been snared in a tender trap of his own making, and he had no one to blame but himself.

# Five

"**B**lythe, where the hell are my brown socks?" Adam raked through the drawer that contained dozens of pairs, tossing socks right and left in his search. "Didn't you wash the darks last night?"

Dammit, he wasn't accustomed to living like this, at the mercy of a very undomestic woman. Since his divorce, he'd had a daily maid, Pearl, who cleaned, did the laundry, the marketing and various mundane chores.

"Look on top of the dryer," Blythe yelled from her bedroom. "I didn't have time to fold anything."

Grumbling under his breath, Adam trudged barefoot from his bedroom to the laundry room. A large wicker basket filled with an unfolded load of towels and washcloths sat atop the dryer. Beside the basket lay a pile of socks. Rummaging through the heap, he found his brown ones.

Three weeks of wedded bliss had just about been the death of him. But what the hell had he expected? A marriage in name only that began without a proper wedding night could hardly bode well for days of contentment and nights of passion.

He was a married man who had had to give up his condo, his maid and his sex life. And for what? For an overly emotional little redhead who wouldn't share his bed, seldom had his meals ready when he came home from work and couldn't be bothered with folding and putting away his socks!

Passing by Blythe's room, he halted and watched her struggling to put her thick mane of short cinnamon hair in order. She forced the brush through it time and again, huffed loudly and threw the brush on the floor.

"Having problems?" he asked.

She jerked her head around and glared at him. "Did you find your socks?"

Holding up the objects in question, he nodded. "You wouldn't have to worry about the laundry if you'd just agree to let Pearl do it when she's here."

"That wasn't part of our agreement," Blythe said. "We agreed to share all the daily household responsibilities, didn't we? How can we do that if you hire a maid to do your part?"

"She'd do your part, too." Bracing his hand on the door frame, he lifted his foot and slipped on one sock. "It's obvious you're not exactly efficient as a housewife, so why should we torture ourselves with my cooking and your lack of time and interest in being a homemaker?"

"I do my share of the cooking, thank you." Blythe stepped into her black leather flats. "But I told you before we got married that I will never be the fetch-your-pipe-and-slippers type of wife, not even for the brief duration of our marriage."

Adam put on his other sock. "Is folding my socks when it's your turn to do the laundry asking for too much? Is preparing a decent meal the nights it's your turn to cook asking for too much? I don't think so."

"I do prepare decent meals! What was wrong with the dinner I cooked last night?" She planted her hands on her hips and glowered at Adam.

"For one thing, it wasn't ready when I came home. And for another thing, our dinner consisted of two microwave chicken dinners and some chocolate chip cookies."

"So?" Her stance and facial expression issued him a dare.

"So, if it has slipped your notice, I'm a pretty big man with a big appetite. One little microwave dinner and a few stale cookies wouldn't fill my hollow leg, let alone appease my hunger."

"The cookies were not stale."

"All these domestic problems could be solved like that—" he snapped his fingers "—if you'd be reasonable and let me get Pearl out here every day. I'm paying her salary to do practically nothing, just keep my condo dusted."

"This isn't a big house and there are only the two of us. We don't really need a maid. If you'd just compromise a bit, make a few concessions—"

"What you want is for me to change my life to suit you," Adam said.

"I'd say it was the other way around." Blythe shoved him out of the way as she walked out of her bedroom and into the hall.

"It's my turn to fix breakfast this morning," she said. "I hope a bowl of Shredded Wheat, a banana and coffee suits you. And it'll be decaf, unless you want to fix yourself a cup of instant."

Adam groaned silently, but didn't say a word. Blythe hurried down the hallway and toward the kitchen. He knew the breakfast she had planned was more nutritious for her and the baby than what he liked—bacon, eggs and biscuits—so he endured their healthy meals, then woofed down his favorites at lunch every day.

Adam had hoped against hope that Blythe might surprise him and turn out to be more interested in making a home for them than in her thriving florist shop. He should have known better. He'd figured her out when they first met two years ago—she was like his mother and his ex-wife.

From the time he'd been a small boy, he had listened to his parents' daily arguments over his mother's lack of interest in their home while she had devoted herself to her secretarial job—a job which eventually led her to a managerial position and marriage to her boss. She'd had no qualms about walking out on her husband and ten-year-old son.

Adam would never forget his father's continuous roar of rage and disillusionment. "I work myself to death trying to build a construction company so I can give you and Adam a good life, and what kind of thanks do I get? Sandwiches instead of hot meals. A son who comes home to an empty house. And a stack of dirty laundry all the way to the ceiling.

"My mother had to work in the fields, picking cotton, and she did all her washing on a washboard, but she still took care of my pa and five kids. She cooked two hot meals every day. So don't you whine to me about not having time to be a good housewife while you pursue a career!"

Adam cringed when he thought about how ill-suited his parents had been for each other and how unrealistic their expectations for each other had been.

When he'd married Lynn, she'd been the old-fashioned girl his father had wanted him to marry. Sweet, obedient, even docile. But then again, Lynn had been only eighteen and fresh off a farm in Cherokee. But exposure to the good life that Adam's money afforded her changed Lynn. And Adam had made concession after concession, trying to be the loving, supportive husband his father hadn't been. He had been determined to save his marriage, to accept his wife's right to a career, but he had drawn the line at infidelity.

Adam went into his bedroom and finished dressing, then joined Blythe in the kitchen. She had set the table, placed his banana by his cereal bowl and had poured his coffee.

"I can fix you some toast to go with that, if it's not enough," she said.

"I'd appreciate that." He picked up the box of Shredded Wheat and filled the bowl. "Four pieces, with butter and jelly."

Blythe scooted back her chair, stood and reached out for the loaf of bread on the counter. She placed four pieces in the toaster, then removed the margarine and grape jelly from the refrigerator.

She supposed she should have realized that a guy as big as Adam couldn't be satisfied with the same size servings she was accustomed to eating. She'd have to remember, from now on, to prepare more food for him.

She wanted this marriage to work for its brief duration. She wanted to become friends with Adam. She wanted to have a cordial, cooperative relationship with her child's father. And Lord knows, she had tried. But sometimes, Adam infuriated her so much she couldn't see straight.

Of course, she had to admit that he was trying, just as hard as she was, to keep things on an even keel. She had suffered through his burned pork chops and he'd suffered through her variety of microwave meals. She'd laughed when his first attempt at washing clothes had ruined the whole wash. He had laundered the darks and lights together, turning the white items a muddy, pinkish brown. And instead of commenting on her lack of housekeeping skills the first week of their marriage, he'd simply written his name in the dust on the coffee table.

Blythe buttered his toast, then spread a thin layer of jelly on each slice, placed them on a plate and handed them to Adam.

"There's really no need for you to take time off from work to go with me to see Dr. Meyers this morning." Blythe sat down at the table and peeled her banana. As she sliced it, she dropped the pieces into her cereal. "He's not doing anything important this month. He won't do the ultrasound until next month."

"Next month is when we find out our baby's sex, isn't it?" Adam devoured a piece of toast in three bites.

"If we want to know."

"Don't you want to find out?" he asked.

"Yes, I suppose so. Especially if I were decorating a nursery."

"I told you to go ahead and decorate the third bedroom. I'll get someone in to move everything out and then you can do whatever you want to the room."

"But that would be a waste of time and money since I . . . we won't be living here."

"I think you and the baby should stay on here after the—" Adam gazed directly at Blythe and found her staring at him. He swallowed. "After our divorce. Until I build you a house of your own."

"That isn't necessary."

"Yes, it is. It's part of our agreement."

"Fine." Blythe wondered if she and Adam were the only newly married couple who sat around at the breakfast table discussing their upcoming divorce.

They finished their breakfast in silence. Blythe gathered up the dishes and placed them in the dishwasher. When she turned around to gather up their cups and spoons, she bumped into Adam, who stood directly behind her. He held their cups and spoons in his hands.

His body pressed against hers. For several minutes she didn't move, couldn't move. She barely breathed. Every time Adam got this close to her, she lost all reason. She tingled from head to toe.

"I'll finish up in here while you get ready," he said. "We don't want you and baby Wyatt to be late for your appointment."

Adam glanced down between them toward her stomach. Blythe leaned backward, her legs pushing against the open dishwasher door. Maneuvering around her, he deposited the cups and spoons into the dishwasher, then slipped his arm about Blythe's waist, pulling her intimately against him. He dropped one hand down to her stomach and spread out his fingers.

Why couldn't things be different? he wondered. Why couldn't his marriage be a love match? He had been Blythe's first lover—her only lover, and she was going to have his child. But she wouldn't have sex with him, wouldn't let him make slow, sweet love to her the way he wanted to do. Three weeks of sleeping under the same roof with a woman he greatly desired had taken its toll on Adam's nerves. How on earth was he going to endure seven more months of celibacy? Five months until the baby was born, then possibly two more months until they signed the divorce papers.

Blythe eased away from Adam, unable to endure his loving touch another moment. She knew he wanted to make love to her, that he was frustrated by her continued refusal to be his lover while they were married.

She didn't dare let Adam make love to her again. Their marriage had already become too real to suit her. Despite being constantly annoyed by her bossy, overbearing husband, she lay awake at night wanting him. If she gave in to her desire, she could very easily find herself falling in love with a man who had every intention of divorcing her after their child was born.

Not that she wanted to stay married to Adam. No way. If she were to remain as Adam's wife for too long, she ran the risk of losing her own identity, of giving in to his ideals. She wouldn't do that. She'd spent her whole life becoming the independent woman her mother never had the courage to become.

She was not going to allow her overwhelming attraction to Adam Wyatt to undermine her principles.

Don't scream, Blythe told herself. Remain calm. Allow Adam to open the door and help you get in his car.

After assisting her, Adam closed the door, rounded the hood and got inside his Lotus. He tossed the stack of booklets onto the floorboard. Leaning over he checked her safety belt, then patted Blythe's stomach.

"Dr. Meyers seemed worried that you haven't gained back the weight you lost when you had so much trouble with morning sickness. That's not good for you or our baby." Adam inserted the key into the ignition.

She was not going to hit him over the head with her purse. She was not going to tell him he had acted like a total fool in the doctor's office. And she most certainly was not going to allow Adam to take charge of every aspect of her life during this pregnancy.

He had asked so many questions that even Dr. Meyers seemed a bit annoyed. What should have been a routine examination, turned out to be an hour of interrogation for her obstetrician and sixty minutes of unnecessary stress for her.

Adam backed his Lotus out of the parking place. "I'm taking you out for an early lunch, and I want you to eat a big, healthy meal. Where would you like to go?"

"I want to go to Petals Plus." She spoke slowly and distinctly, forcing herself to remain calm. "Joy will want to go home by twelve, and this afternoon I'm interviewing potential part-time employees. Remember? It was your idea. Not mine. I think I can continue handling things without extra help for another month, until the Christmas season."

"I'll call Joy and see if she can stay another hour, and if you'd like I can do the interviews for you. You should probably go home and take a nap. Dr. Meyers said mothers-to-be need extra rest." He pulled out of the parking lot and onto the street.

"I get plenty of rest." Blythe stared straight ahead, determined not to look at Adam. If she did, she might lose control and say some things she'd regret later. "And I will do the interviews and choose my own employees. You don't know the first thing about running a florist shop."

"You're angry with me, aren't you?"

Clenching her teeth, she closed her eyes and prayed for strength. "I am not angry." She enunciated every word of her untruthful statement. "A little upset, perhaps, but not angry."

"Look, I know I might have gone a bit overboard with all my questions for Dr. Meyers, but—"

"A bit overboard? Ha!"

"I think he understood that I'm a concerned father, who wants to be involved in every aspect of this pregnancy."

"You're involved, dammit! You're involved! You watch every bite that goes into my mouth. You double-check to make sure I'm taking my vitamin and mineral supplements. You bought every book on the subject of pregnancy and childbirth ever printed and you expect me to read all of them, too."

"Calm down. You're getting upset over nothing." Adam glanced at her and saw that her cheeks had turned a bright pink. She might deny her anger, but she couldn't hide the evidence. "We'll do whatever you want. I'll drive you over to Petals Plus so Joy can go home, then I'll run over to Court Street Café and get lunch for us. You like their grilled shrimp and rice, don't you?"

Letting out a long, deep breath, Blythe relaxed her shoulders and nodded her head. How could she stay angry at a man who tried so hard to please her? "You don't have to eat lunch with me. You've already taken off work all morning."

"I want us to have lunch together," he said. "We can discuss the reception."

Blythe groaned. "Is the reception really necessary?"

"It's going to look odd if we don't have one. After all, my friends and business associates will expect it. And so will yours. Since we had such a small, private wedding, a few people will feel snubbed if we don't have a large reception."

"Next week, huh?" Blythe dreaded the thought of being put on display in front of Adam's friends.

"It's all set. My secretary sent the invitations out last week. I told you. Don't you remember?"

"Yes, I remember," she said, then mumbled under her breath, "but I'd like to forget."

Adam drove past Lloyd's Drugstore and up Second Avenue, parking directly in front of Petals Plus. Blythe didn't wait for him to open her door. She got out and headed straight for her shop, leaving him to follow.

"How's mother and baby?" Joy asked when Blythe stormed in, Adam right on her heels.

"We're fine," Blythe said. "But the father isn't!"

"Uh-oh. What happened?" Joy glanced from Blythe to Adam. "Let me guess. You went in with Blythe to see Dr. Meyers and you questioned him on every aspect of Blythe's care."

"Oh, he did that all right." Blythe stomped into the back room, threw down her purse on the battered wooden desk and jerked her bright pink smock off the brass peg. As she walked out of the storeroom-makeshift office, she slipped into her smock.

"Ask him what he knows about the fetus at the end of the third month." Crossing her arms over her chest, Blythe patted her foot on the floor.

Staring wide-eyed at her friend, Joy smiled. Grinning, Adam shook his head.

"Go ahead," Blythe demanded. "Ask him!"

"Pacify her," Adam said. "She's upset with me because I acted like a possessive, protective husband and father."

"Oh, I see," Joy said. "Well, tell me, Adam, what do you know about your baby?"

"I know that she—or he—is about three inches long and weighs less than an ounce, but already she—" he glanced at Blythe, who had uncrossed her arms and stuck her hands into the two deep side pockets in her smock "—or he—has fingernails and toenails, the bones have begun to calcify, the sex organs are developing and so are the tooth buds in the mouth. The muscles of the—"

"Good grief, that's enough." Blythe huffed loudly. "See what I'm up against? The man is a walking encyclopedia on pregnancy. He knows more about it than I do!"

Adam looked at Joy, a comical look of suppliance on his face. "I'm going to run over to Court Street Café and pick up some lunch for us. Can you stay and eat with us?"

"My baby-sitter has to leave by twelve-thirty," Joy said. "I'm afraid I'll have go home and make myself a sandwich."

"Well, while I'm gone, how about talking to my wife on my behalf and convincing her I'm acting fairly normal for a first-time, expectant father?"

"I'll see what I can do."

"Thanks." Adam stared at Blythe, who refused to look his way. "Do you want the grilled shrimp?"

"Yes," she replied, then turned her back to him. "And get me a piece of their New York cheesecake."

"That may be a little rich for you, and it's filled with way too much fat. Maybe you should choose a different—"

Joy cleared her throat loudly. Adam sucked in his breath, and nodded to her, understanding her warning.

"I'll get us both the cheesecake for dessert," Adam said and hurried out the front door.

The moment he left, Blythe blew out a loud breath and slumped down on the stool at her work counter behind a decorative wooden-and-cloth screen.

Joy patted Blythe on the back. "He is acting somewhat normal for a first-time father-to-be. Craig was a raving lunatic the whole time I was pregnant. Some men, the ones who really want to be fathers, go a little overboard sometimes. And a take-charge guy like Adam is bound to go about impending fatherhood the way he does everything else in his life."

"I suppose I'm making a mountain out of a molehill," Blythe admitted. "It's just that I'm not accustomed to sharing my life with a man, to having a husband I have to report in to all the time."

"It works both ways, you know," Joy said. "Adam isn't used to making compromises. He always told Craig that he never intended to remarry. Maybe, if you'd consider his side of the situation, you might realize that this marriage-in-name-only is as difficult for him as it is for you."

"I suppose he's been complaining to Craig about having to remain celibate."

"Craig hasn't mentioned it." Joy smiled coyly.

"Well, Adam agreed . . . we both agreed not to have sex with anyone else while we were legally man and wife."

"And I'm sure Adam will uphold his part of the agreement." Joy clucked her tongue against the roof of her mouth. "But it must be difficult for a man as . . . as sexual as Adam to live in the same house with a woman who is his wife and not be allowed to even touch her."

"He touches me," Blythe said. "He touches me all the time. He's always slipping his arm around my waist and patting my stomach."

Joy grinned. "To be honest, I don't see how you could live with a guy as fabulous as Adam Wyatt and not take advantage of the opportunity to sleep in his bed every night. After all, he is your husband."

"Temporarily. Just until after my six-week checkup. That's when we'll make plans to see the lawyer."

"A lot can happen between now and then."

"What do you mean by that?" Narrowing her eyes to slits, Blythe stared quizzically at Joy.

"Maybe you and Adam will work out your differences and discover that neither of you has to drastically change in order for the two of you to be compatible."

"I seriously doubt that."

"What are you so afraid of?" Joy asked.

"I'm not afraid of any—"

"Don't lie to me. I'm your best friend. I know you. Remember?"

"I'm not going to fall in love with Adam." Blythe's voice was a mere whisper.

"Oh, I see. So that's what you're afraid of, huh?" Grasping Blythe's shoulders, Joy tenderly massaged her tense muscles. "Falling in love isn't something we can control. It just happens. That's why they call it falling. It's like an accident we can't prevent. Just look at Craig and me. I swore I'd never marry some sophisticated smooth talker who came from the same background I did. You know how I always dated the bad boys in school, just to give my father heart failure."

Blythe laughed. "Oh, Lord, do I ever remember. We were always attracted to different types, weren't we? You wanted a Mr. Macho Stud and I wanted a—"

"A guy who was the exact opposite of your stepfather."

Sighing, Blythe nodded. "You know Adam is determined to have a wedding reception at the country club. The invitations went out last week."

"We got ours, but I didn't want to say anything until you mentioned it."

"Everyone's going to know why he married me," Blythe said. "I'll bet half of Decatur already knows. Adam certainly hasn't made a secret of it."

"So, big whoop. All you have to do is stand at Adam's side and smile. Believe me, if anyone so much as dares to utter a questionable remark, Adam will annihilate them. There are times when it's kind of nice to have a big, protective man take care of you."

"You don't know how much I dread the reception. All of Adam's rich business friends will be there, and probably a whole horde of his former girlfriends who'll be trying to figure out why I was lucky enough to snare Adam in the tender trap when none of them could."

"I'd say the answer is obvious."

"How's that?"

"No other woman ever got Adam Wyatt so hot and bothered to make love to her that he completely forgot to use protection."

Blythe gnawed on her bottom lip. "I wish..."

"What do you wish?"

Blythe had been about to say that she wished she could forget that night, wished she could stop remembering the way she'd felt, the way Adam had made her feel. Just thinking about all the things he'd said and done—the things she'd said and done—created a draining ache inside her.

"I wish Adam would hurry up with our lunch. I'm starving."

# Six

Blythe shifted from one foot to the other, wondering if the reception line had an end or if it would go on forever. She tried to smile when Adam introduced her to yet another business associate and his dowdy middle-aged wife, who surveyed Blythe from head to toe, her gaze resting meaningfully on Blythe's stomach.

She sucked in her stomach, but it didn't do any good. Trying to camouflage a thickening waistline and a little round tummy was impossible on a five-foot-two woman who was over four months pregnant.

"So nice to meet you, my dear," the woman said, lifting her gaze to stare directly into Blythe's face. "We'd given up hope of Adam ever remarrying. You must be quite special to have snared such a confirmed bachelor. Surely you know how lucky you are."

Adam slipped his arm around Blythe's waist and hugged her to his side. "I've never known anyone as special as

Blythe. And I'm the lucky one, Wylodean, to have this lovely lady as my wife."

"I agree with you there," Chester McCorkle said, taking in every inch of Blythe's petite body with one quick glance. "Hope you two will be as happy as Wylodean and I have been all these years."

The McCorkles moved on and another couple extended their hands and voiced their best wishes in a cordial greeting.

Blythe's feet hurt. Adam had suggested she not wear the heels she'd bought to match her new outfit, but she'd insisted. She wanted to look perfect when he put her on display at this reception. How could she look perfect in flats, with her head barely reaching Adam's shoulder? She knew his friends and associates were all wealthy, important people. She didn't want to disappoint him when tonight obviously meant so much to him. She felt that she owed him this night, especially after the way he'd been doing his best to make their unholy alliance as easy for her as possible.

She sighed with relief the moment she saw Joy and Craig, and behind them several of her business acquaintances from Decatur's Downtown Merchants' Association. Finally, she'd be able to talk to someone she knew.

Joy threw her arms around Blythe. "You look fabulous. You're the only redhead I know who can wear pink." Blythe whispered her next statement. "That outfit must have cost a fortune."

"Adam insisted I spare no expense when I chose something for tonight," Blythe told her best friend in a hushed tone. "If I'd been showing more, I'd have had to buy a maternity dress."

"You two are holding up the line," Craig said. "Come on, Joy. You and Blythe can talk later."

"Hang in there." Joy squeezed Blythe's hand. "And you're not showing."

Adam glanced at his wife—his bride of one month—and his chest swelled with pride. Blythe was a lovely, enchanting woman, and never more so than she was tonight, four months pregnant with his child.

And Joy was right about her being able to wear pink quite well, despite her dark, cinnamon hair. The three-piece muted pink outfit she'd chosen made her eyes look greener and her auburn hair a light mahogany. The lace cardigan was sheer and easily revealed the low-cut silk blouse beneath. Adam swallowed. Blythe's small, pert breasts had enlarged. Every time he looked at her, he wondered in what other ways her breasts had changed.

The full skirt, that subtly hid her tiny, rounded belly was some sort of floral lace and hit her about two inches above her knees, showing off her great legs.

Adam's body hardened at the thought of those slim legs wrapped around him, holding him close as he moved in and out of her. Sweat broke out on his upper lip. Damn! He had to get his mind off making love to his wife or he'd embarrass them both if he stood there, obviously aroused while greeting their guests.

Adam glanced down the line and sighed with relief when he realized the end was near. Less than a dozen people to go. Thank God. Then he noticed Angela Wright. How the hell did that woman get an invitation? Surely, he hadn't put her name on the list. He had dated Angela for several months and had decided to call it quits before Missy Simpson's christening party, but hadn't gotten around to ending things until afterward. After he'd slept with Blythe. After he'd gotten her pregnant the first time they made love.

Angela hadn't wanted to end things. She'd been too possessive, too clinging to suit Adam. He'd known all along that she wanted more than he could give her, and that, to her, his most attractive asset was his bank account.

Blythe noticed the ravishing blond in the skintight, bleached-blue-denim-and-lace strapless dress. The daring bustier style lifted and exposed a large portion of her Playmate-of-the-Year-size breasts.

Who was the woman? Blythe wondered. She certainly wasn't a friend or acquaintance of hers. She must be an old *friend* of Adam's. One of his former girlfriends, no doubt!

"Adam, darling!" The statuesque blond threw her arms around Adam, shoving her big, partially uncovered breasts against his chest as she kissed him passionately on the mouth.

Blythe's stomach did an evil flip-flop, the sensation identical to the one a person gets during the descent of a too fast Ferris wheel. She knotted her hands into tight fists to prevent herself from ripping the blonde off Adam.

Adam tried to push Angela away, but she clung to him, nuzzling the side of his face with her cheek. "Aren't you the naughty boy, getting married on the sly like you did. And after you swore you'd never marry again."

Oh, God! Adam closed his eyes and said a quick, silent prayer that Angela wouldn't make a scene. He wanted tonight to be perfect for Blythe. He had thought he could show her how proud he was to present her to the world as his bride.

"I found a woman who changed my mind," Adam said, then gave Angela another gentle shove, trying to dislodge himself from her tenacious hold.

"Well, you must introduce us. I've been simply dying to meet the woman who reeled you in." With one arm still laced through Adam's, Angela turned sharply and glared at Blythe. "Is this her? My goodness, she's not at all what I expected."

"Angela . . ." Adam warned.

"As you can see, Adam's tastes have changed." Blythe's lips curved into her best eat-dirt-and-die smile. "For the better."

Adam strangled, then coughed several times to clear his throat.

Blythe uncurled her tight fist and extended her hand to Angela. "Since Adam seems to have lost his powers of

speech for the moment, let me introduce myself. I'm
Adam's wife, Blythe Elliott Wyatt. And you're . . . ?''

Shaking Blythe's hand, Angela grinned. ''I'm a dear old
friend of your husband's.'' Angela released Blythe's hand
and tiptoed her fingers up the front of Adam's white tuxedo shirt. She turned her heated gaze on Blythe. ''You simply must tell me your secret, sweetie. How did you trap this
big guy into marriage when better women have tried and
failed?''

Adam's face turned scarlet. The area within a twelve-foot
radius around the reception line went deadly quiet, only the
clatter of champagne glasses, the murmurs of the crowd and
the upbeat tune the band played could be heard at a distance.

Blythe grabbed Angela's wrist, jerking her hand away
from Adam's chest. ''I suppose I could deny that I trapped
him, but I won't.'' Blythe gave the larger woman's arm a not
so gentle yank, removing the blonde from her intimate position against Adam. ''And I could say that I tried a trap
that had been used successfully time and again, but
that's what you probably did, without success. No, you
see I snagged Adam with a brand-new, never-before-used
trap . . . but without his total cooperation, indeed his blind
passion, even my virgin trap wouldn't have caught him.''

Glancing at Adam, who stood with his mouth agape,
Angela giggled nervously. ''Feisty little thing isn't she, darling?''

Blythe stepped between her husband and his former
girlfriend. Leaning her small body back against Adam, she
glared up at Angela. ''And she's possessive and jealous,
too,'' Blythe said. ''What's mine is mine. I don't share.''

Angela glanced around at the silent crowd of onlookers.
''You certainly don't mind making a spectacle of yourself
and embarrassing Adam in front of his friends, do you?''

Slipping his arms around Blythe, Adam rested his chin on
the top of her head. ''I'm not the least embarrassed,'' he
said.

Blythe took a deep breath. She held up her left hand directly in front of Angela's face. "As long as this ring is on my finger, Adam Wyatt belongs to me. Do you understand?"

"It doesn't matter whether Angela understands or not, sweetheart," Adam said. "I understand."

Angela turned sharply and marched toward the exit, not daring to look back or to respond to the people who spoke to her.

Wylodean McCorkle pranced up to Blythe and Adam, her round, wrinkled face splotched with vivid color. "Well, I never! What a disgraceful show!" She patted a trembling Blythe on the shoulder. "Well done, my dear. I've never seen a wife make hash of a troublemaking mistress with such adept ease." Narrowing her eyes, she zeroed in on Adam. "You're right. You are the lucky one."

"Former mistress," Adam said.

"What?" Wylodean asked.

"I ended my association with Angela before Blythe and I married."

"And a good thing you did," Wylodean said.

Blythe suddenly felt light-headed. Of all the problems she had expected to encounter tonight, a one-on-one with Adam's former *mistress* had never entered her mind.

She couldn't seem to stop trembling. And Lord knew how high her blood pressure had shot. She was still trying to figure out exactly why she had publicly laid claim to Adam Wyatt the way she had. Anyone here would think she was madly in love with the man. The truth was that she was just plain mad.

And in her anger, she had practically announced to the world that she'd been a virgin who had trapped Adam into marriage by getting herself pregnant.

*Oh, dear Lord!*

"Blythe, are you all right?" Joy nudged Wylodean McCorkle out of the way. "I swear, if I'd had a gun I'd have shot that bitch. But it would take an elephant gun to blow her away.''

Blythe laughed, but the sound came out a hoarse squeak.

"I'm going to be sick," Blythe said.

"What?" Adam twirled her around to face him. "I thought that morning sickness stuff ended last month."

"How dare you invite that woman to our wedding reception!" Blythe bit the words out between clenched teeth, her voice a rasping whisper.

"I didn't—"

"If you ever see that woman again, I'll...I'll..."

Adam grinned. "I promise that—"

"If you even see her out somewhere, you'd better cross the street to avoid her. Do I make myself clear?"

"Perfectly clear, Mrs. Wyatt."

"Wipe that ridiculous smile off your face, you big baboon!" Blythe burst into tears and ran from the room.

Joy caught up with her inside the ladies' room. "Are you all right?" Joy wrapped her arms around Blythe.

Blythe sobbed against Joy's shoulder. "I just made a complete fool of myself out there over a man who doesn't love me."

"You did no such thing. You did what any red-blooded American woman would have done. You warned off a scavenger. You let her know you weren't some little docile wifey who would look the other way."

"How could he have invited that woman?"

"I don't think he did," Joy said. "Angela Wright is the type who'd crash a party."

Pulling out of Joy's arms, Blythe wiped her eyes with her fingers and took a deep breath. "Do you know her?"

"I met her a few times when Adam was dating her."

"How serious was their relationship?" Blythe asked.

"Not any more serious than any other relationship Adam has had since his divorce. Angela was a nice ornament for Adam's arm and a willing bed partner, but even before

Missy's christening, he'd told Craig he planned to end things with the woman."

"She really is gorgeous, isn't she?" Blythe looked in the mirror and groaned when she saw her smeared makeup. "Why would any man settle for this—" she pivoted around slowly, as if on display "—if he could have her?"

"This insecurity isn't like you," Joy said. "You're one of the most self-confident people I've ever known. Something's wrong here. Confess. What is it?"

"I don't know what you're talking about."

"Sure you do. You've gone and fallen in love with Adam Wyatt. That display of possessiveness out there wasn't for show."

"You're crazy."

"No, I'm not crazy. But *you* are in love."

"I am not. I can't be. It has to be something else. I'm pregnant and my hormones are all screwed up. That's got to be it." Blythe turned on the lavatory faucets, caught a double handful of water and splashed it in her face. "I'll have to redo my makeup before I go back out there. Would you mind finding Adam and letting him know I'm all right?"

Sighing, Joy nodded. "Take all the time you need. I'll go talk to your husband."

Adam had decided that he'd never be able to figure out women in general and Blythe in particular. Joy had explained Blythe's tearful outburst as nothing more than pregnancy hormones, and he had no choice but to agree, especially when Blythe returned to the reception with a smile on her face. She'd wooed and won his friends and associates with her intelligence and charm. He'd been so proud of her he could have burst, and his male ego had been inflated by her rather primitive display of possessiveness.

In the back of his mind, he'd thought that tonight just might be the night his celibate marriage would end. After all, not having sex had been Blythe's idea, not his.

But the moment they were alone in his Lotus, all his dreams of bliss had been destroyed by five little words— *Why did you invite her?*

After ten minutes of trying to convince Blythe that Angela had either crashed the party or had come with someone who had received an invitation, he'd given up. They had driven home in silence—a heavy, dark silence that seemed endless. But he was smart enough to know when to shut up, to realize when arguing was useless. He had, without a doubt, married the most stubborn woman on the face of the earth. And the most jealous.

The minute he parked the Lotus, Blythe jumped out of the car and fled into the house. Adam took his time getting out. Cursing under his breath, he deliberated whether or not he should turn around and drive back into Decatur and spend the night at his condo. He wasn't sure what to expect when he walked through the front door. Would Blythe continue giving him the silent treatment or would she blast him with false accusations again?

Hell, he couldn't run away. He had agreed to this fake marriage for the duration of Blythe's pregnancy and recovery period. No matter what, he had to uphold his end of the bargain and see this thing through to the end.

When he entered the living room, he found it empty. She must have gone straight to her bedroom. Adam took off his tuxedo jacket, removed his black bow tie and undid the buttons on his white shirt. He walked down the hall toward his own room, but when he passed Blythe's room, she stepped out into the hall.

Planting her hands on her hips, she glared at him. "I believe you if you say you didn't invite her." Blythe turned sharply, went back into her room and closed the door with a resounding wham.

"I'll be damned." Adam laughed. Women were a mystery to him, and his own spitfire of a wife was the biggest puzzle of them all.

He grabbed the doorknob to her bedroom door, intending to march right in, then thought better of the idea and knocked loudly.

"What?" she asked through the closed door.

"May I come in?"

"It's late, and I'm tired. We'll talk in the morning."

"Blythe, if you're willing to listen, I'll tell you about Angela."

Silence. Utter, absolute silence.

"Blythe?"

The door swung open and there she stood, her back ramrod straight, her hazel eyes ablaze and her soft little jaw tightly clamped.

Adam stepped over the threshold, walked up to Blythe and smiled at her. She quivered ever so slightly. Reaching out, he caressed her cheek with his fingertips. She closed her eyes and drew in a deep breath.

"I dated Angela for a few months," he said. "We had a brief affair, and—"

"Oh." Blythe's eyes flew open. She moved backward, trying to escape Adam's caressing fingers.

He clasped her neck gently, pulling her closer—so close his breath mingled with hers. She shivered. "Angela wanted me for my money. Plain and simple. And I made it perfectly clear from the very beginning that I wasn't interested in a permanent relationship, most certainly not marriage."

"Were you still dating her the night you and I...the night we—"

"The night we made love. The night you gave me your virginity. The night I gave you my child."

Dropping her chin, Blythe lowered her eyes to the carpeted floor. "Yes, that night. Were you still dating her?"

"I had decided to end things with her before Missy's christening, but I didn't officially break things off until after the night we were together."

"Did you see her again during those two months before I told you I was pregnant?"

"Yes, I saw her again." Adam gripped Blythe's chin and lifted her face. "To officially end our affair."

"She thinks she has some sort of claim on you."

"You're the only woman who has any kind of claim on me."

Blythe laid her hand over her belly. "This child is my only claim on you."

He took her into his arms—his wife, the mother of his child—lifted her off her feet and kissed her lips with tenderness. While she was still swaying from the sweet gentle passion of his kiss, Adam scooped her up into his arms, carried her to her bed and sat down, settling her on his lap.

"During those two months after you spent the night at my condo, I dated a dozen different women," Adam admitted.

Blythe squirmed on his lap, averting her gaze so she wouldn't have to look at him. "I figured as much."

"Did you figure that I'd date a dozen different lovely and very willing women and not have sex with any of them?"

Blythe sat up very straight and stared at Adam, her full pink mouth opening into a slanted oval as she sucked in her breath. "I—I... You didn't? But why?"

"The hell if I know," Adam said. "Maybe some fiery little redheaded virgin ruined me for other women."

"You're kidding me?" Blythe smiled, then giggled.

"What's so damned funny?" he asked.

"I was that good, huh? And to think, I didn't have the vaguest idea what I was doing. I just acted on instinct." She draped her arm around his neck.

Grinning, Adam tossed them both backward onto the bed. They landed with a bounce. "You knocked me for a loop, babe. Just think how remarkable you'd be with a little practice."

"Hey, buster, just hold on one minute." She shoved against his chest, but he trapped her hands between them when he pulled her body up against his.

He nuzzled her nose. "Why don't you admit that you enjoyed our night together as much as I did?"

"I've never denied that I enjoyed being... having... doing... Oh, shoot, you know what I'm trying to say."

He eased her lace cardigan off her shoulders and kissed the freckles spread across her taut skin like bronze glitter on ivory parchment. "No, Blythe, why don't you tell me what you're trying to say. Put your feelings into words. Take a chance. Make a giant confession the way I did."

"What sort of giant confession did you make?" She moaned when he slid his hand up her leg and caressed her thigh.

"I haven't been with another woman since the night I made love to you." Rising over her, Adam braced his big body with his arms placed on each side of her, then he lowered his head and covered her mouth, thrusting his tongue between her sigh-parted lips.

At first she merely accepted his kiss, totally consumed by Adam's masterful domination. But when her body came alive, tingling with sexual urgency, she returned the kiss. Within minutes, the same wild, raw hunger that had driven them to the very edge of sanity the first time they'd made love surged through them with blinding force.

Breathless, Adam released her lips and groaned. "I want you so much. Every time I look at you, I want to rip off your clothes and take you. Do you have any idea how I've fantasized about lifting you onto the kitchen table during breakfast and taking you right then and there?"

Blythe felt as if her breath was trapped in her lungs. Her chest ached. Her throat tightened. Her body throbbed with a powerful need to have this man inside her.

"Please, don't do this to me. Don't make me want you when we both know we don't have a future together."

"Dammit, Blythe, why can't you just be honest and admit that we're good together? Hell, we're great together. We set the sheets on fire the night we made love." Lowering his body, he pressed himself against her, rubbing his hardness against her feminine mound. "You're my wife. I want you."

She tried to push him away, but he wouldn't budge. "I'm not really your wife, Adam, and we both know it. We have a business agreement. Nothing more."

"Oh, we have a lot more than a business agreement, and you damn well know it." He rose up and rolled off her, then sat on the edge of her bed. "Tonight at the reception, I thought I was finally getting a glimpse of the real Blythe Elliott—the real woman. The woman who staked a claim on her man. That strong, possessive woman wouldn't run scared."

Blythe's chest rose and fell with her labored breathing. She lay flat on her back on the bed, staring up at the ceiling. "Why don't you just accept the fact that I am not now nor ever will be the *real* woman you want me to be? You can't accept me for who I am, and I have no intention of changing my ideals or giving up my identity to please you."

A lone tear escaped Blythe's eye, slid downward past her ear and onto the pastel quilt.

"I didn't ask you to change your ideals." Adam stood, his back facing her. "And heaven forbid you should do anything to please me. After all, I don't mean a thing to you, do I?"

That's not true, she wanted to shout. You mean far too much to me. I'm falling in love with you, and if I don't protect myself you'll break my heart.

He walked across the room, then hesitated momentarily in the open doorway and glanced back at her. She didn't look up at him. "Just tell me one thing, babe. What was that all about at the reception tonight, that outraged wife bit, that jealous, possessive woman who staked a claim on me? Was it all an act?"

Blythe tried to speak, but tears caught in her throat, choking her. Adam walked out into the hall and slammed her bedroom door behind him.

Turning over, Blythe jerked up a pillow and buried her face in it. Muffling her broken sobs, she cried until she was spent, then curled into a ball and closed her eyes. How would she ever get any sleep tonight when all she wanted to do was run across the hall and throw herself into Adam's arms? But she couldn't. She didn't dare. Regardless of the passion that sprang to life between them whenever they touched, Adam didn't love her and hadn't offered her a lifetime commitment. All he wanted was for them to be lovers during their brief marriage of necessity. For him it was a simple matter of needing a woman. For her, it was a complicated matter of needing love and acceptance.

Adam undressed, threw back the covers and crawled into bed, naked. He ached. His hard body throbbed with need. Dammit, why was Blythe being so stubborn about their making love again? She wanted him as much as he wanted her. Hell! Did she get some perverse sense of pleasure out of torturing him?

Maybe she'd been able to control her desire tonight, but sooner or later a woman as passionate as Blythe was bound to give in to her primitive wants and needs. He just hoped he didn't die of frustration before she realized she was fighting a losing battle.

# Seven

The baby fluttered inside Blythe's womb. She gripped the glass of orange juice in her trembling hand and slowly set it down on the table.

"Is something wrong?" Adam asked, glancing over the morning newspaper he held in front of him.

"No, nothing's wrong. I'm fine." She should tell him that their child was moving. She should take his hand and lay it over her stomach so that he could feel the miracle growing inside her. But she couldn't bear the thought of Adam touching her, of sharing such an intimate moment with him. She'd first felt the slight stirrings nearly a dozen days ago, but she had told no one, not even Joy.

"You look pale." He folded the newspaper and laid it on the table. "Are you sure you're all right?"

"I said I'm fine!" Damn, why did she always snap his head off over the most innocent comments? "I'm sorry, Adam, I suppose I'm just a bit nervous about my doctor's appointment this afternoon."

"But Dr. Meyers said that there's no danger in having a sonogram done," Adam assured her. "What was it he said when I asked about any risks? Oh, yes. He said that in twenty-five years there had been no known risks."

"I'm not worried about the sonogram, just excited and nervous, wondering exactly what we'll be able to see." The baby was becoming more and more real every day. She could feel the tiny life moving inside her, and today she would see her child for the first time.

"Why don't you take the morning off and just rest and relax?" Adam suggested.

"I can't do that. This is December, one of my busiest months."

"If you'd hired extra help the way I wanted you to do, you'd be able to take a day off now and then, and you wouldn't have to work so hard."

"I haven't found anyone suitable," Blythe said.

"You haven't interviewed anyone for the last three weeks. It isn't a good idea to wait around to the last minute to hire someone reliable to take over when you have the baby."

Adam had never known anyone so determined to run a business single-handedly. He sometimes wondered just what Blythe was trying to prove, and to whom.

He had a surprise for her this morning, one she might not want, but one she needed. She'd probably throw a royal fit at first and pout at him for a day or two, but he could deal with both as long as she forgave him and realized he'd done what was best for her and the baby.

"I'll get around to finding someone."

The baby moved again and Blythe gasped. She glanced across the table at her husband, who glared at her.

"There is something wrong? What is it? Are you in pain?" He scooted back his chair.

"Sit down and finish your coffee. I am perfectly all right," she told him.

Adam nodded agreement, pulled his chair back up to the table and picked up his cup. He had no idea what was going on, but something was causing Blythe's odd actions this morning. He chuckled under his breath, then took a swig of coffee. Why should this morning be any different than the rest of the time? Most of his wife's actions seemed a bit odd to him. She constantly surprised him, often amazed him, and occasionally infuriated him. But she always aroused him. Living with Blythe, having her so near all the time, was like being fifteen and having a crush on a beautiful young teacher you saw every day, but was never allowed to touch.

He hadn't been this sexually frustrated since he'd been a teenager, and God knew he'd never been celibate for four months. Why was it that since his divorce from Lynn, he'd been able to pick and choose women on his own terms—until Blythe? And when things ended, he'd had no regrets. But Blythe was different. He'd known she was different the first time they met. That was one of the reasons he'd stayed away from her. And that was the reason he had forgotten to use protection the first time he'd made love to her—the reason she was pregnant with his child.

He had known women more beautiful, more voluptuous and far more experienced. But he had never known anyone quite like Blythe Elliott. She created a need inside him that only she could satisfy. An ache that only she could appease.

"Have you put in a bid on the River Walk project?" Blythe asked, then peeled a banana and dumped its skin onto her empty plate.

"What?"

"Last night you were telling me about all the new construction possibilities in the Decatur area, about how now more than ever before, your firm had a chance to bid on projects right here at home." She took a bite out of the banana.

He liked being able to discuss business with Blythe. Most of the women he'd dated hadn't had a head for business and found any discussions about his firm terribly boring. Maybe because she owned and managed a business herself, Blythe understood his devotion to his work, his excitement in undertaking a new project. The first time she had made a couple of suggestions, he had ignored her. But after giving her ideas some thought, he realized his wife was a pretty smart businesswoman.

"Construction is fast becoming big business around here," Adam said. "Not just with the River Walk project, but with the new water treatment plant, the new bridge over the Tennessee River, and future plans to build a civic center as well as rebuild the old marina."

"That's certainly more work than one firm could handle," Blythe said. "You know, if you do bid on the River Walk project and win the bid, would you consider using me as one of your subcontractors?"

"You? For what?"

"For landscape design," she told him. "There isn't much I don't know about plants, flowers, shrubs, trees, grass. And I've always wanted to expand, to own and operate a nursery as well as my downtown florist shop."

"How will you have time to run two businesses and raise a child?"

She felt as if he'd reached across the table and slapped her. She had never shared her dreams with anyone except Joy. Now she'd shared them with Adam. She'd been foolish to think he'd understand, that he might actually encourage her. What had she expected him to say? *"Why, honey, that's a great idea. What can I do to help you? And of course, I'll consider you for a subcontracting job if Wyatt Construction wins the River Walk bid."*

He knew by the expression on her face that he'd said the wrong thing. What surprised him was that she hadn't already blasted him with that little viper tongue of hers. But no, she just sat there staring at him, her jaw tight, her lips closed, her breathing quickening with every breath. He had found out from living with her for two months now that Blythe was far more dangerous when she was quiet than when she was vocal.

"How are you killing me this time?" he asked. "Boiling me in oil? Tossing me into shark-infested waters? Or perhaps feeding me to a man-eating plant?"

"What are you talking about?"

"Don't think you can fool me. Every time you get that look on your face, I know you're fantasizing about ways to murder me."

Blythe's lips twitched ever so slightly as she tried not to smile. Damn the man! He had a knack for making her angry, but an even greater talent for making her laugh.

"You really don't want to know the answer to your question. It's better for you not to know my fantasies." And it was better for her if he didn't know them, because more often than not, she wasn't plotting his demise, but daydreaming about making love to him.

He reached across the table and took her hand. She stiffened at his touch, but didn't try to pull away from him. His big hand completely encompassed her smaller one.

"I'd like to know all your dreams, all your fantasies, especially if they involve me." He stroked the top of her hand with his thumb, loving the feel of her soft skin. She was soft like that all over, even softer and more delicate in some places. Places he wished he could touch right now.

"I tried to share one of my dreams with you, but you—"

"Questioned your ability to be a mother and a businesswoman." He lifted her hand to his lips, kissing her sweet flesh with tender passion. "I try damn hard not to be such a chauvinist, babe, but sometimes I fail."

She couldn't bear the way his lips burned into her skin, hot and damp and exciting. "If you can run a multimillion-dollar business and be a good father, why couldn't I run a florist and a nursery and be a good mother?"

He inserted his tongue between her index and middle fingers, moving it slowly in and out. Blythe jerked her hand away, stunned by the sensuality of his caress.

Smiling, knowing damn well how he'd made her feel, Adam looked at her with his piercing black eyes, and Blythe tingled from head to toe. How was she going to be able to resist this man for six more months, when every time he came near her, she wanted to throw herself into his arms?

"You're right," he said.

"I am? You mean you agree with me?"

"Sure. In order to be good parents, both of us will have to make concessions, and there will be times when we will have to put our child's needs before our business concerns. Me—" he pointed to himself, and then to her "—as well as you."

"We haven't really discussed exactly how we're going to go about sharing custody of—" The baby moved again. Blythe forced herself not to cover her stomach with her hand. "I mean, well... How can we possibly have equal custody the first six months to a year if I plan on breast-feeding?"

Breast-feed? Had he heard her correctly? She hadn't said anything about breast-feeding. Adam glanced at her high, round breasts and swallowed hard.

The night he'd made love to her in his condo, he had caressed her beautiful little breasts. He had teased her tight pink nipples and tormented them with his mouth until she had cried out for mercy.

Since their wedding night he had wanted to see her breasts, to feel them, taste them.

"You're going to breast-feed our baby?" he asked.

"Yes, I am. Dr. Meyers says it's much healthier for me and the baby, and it's something I really want to do."

"I think that's wonderful. But I never thought you would. I mean, most women don't. Not anymore. Do they?"

"Some women do, and not always the sweet, docile, old-fashioned type you might expect." Blythe scooted back her chair and stood. "Independent, intelligent women breast-feed their babies, too, you know. Just because I have a mind of my own, a business of my own and ideals of my own, doesn't mean I'm not capable of being maternal."

Before she exited the kitchen, he grabbed her shoulder. She halted, but didn't turn to face him.

"The baby will live with you for the entire first year." Lowering his mouth to her ear, he whispered. "I'll want to visit, every day, and maybe even watch you nurse our child."

The image of him standing beside a rocking chair where she sat with their baby at her breast flashed through Blythe's mind. Her breasts tightened. Her nipples pointed. She closed her eyes, savoring the moment.

Adam slipped his arm around her. She shivered.

He could picture their child at her breast, and he could see himself lifting the sleeping infant from Blythe's arms and laying him—or her—down in a cradle. Then he would turn to Blythe, her breasts still bare, swoop her into his arms and carry her to their bed. He could see droplets of sweet mother's milk beading on her nipples. He'd lower his head and capture them with his tongue.

His body shook with desire. He cursed under his breath. His sex hardened painfully, pulsating against Blythe's buttocks. There was no way he could disguise his arousal, no way he could keep her from feeling his desire.

He wanted to take her. Here. Now. Standing up. From behind. She was so tiny, he could lift her effortlessly.

"I—I have to go to work, and...so...do you," Blythe said breathlessly.

He surrounded her petite body with both of his arms, laying his left hand over her slightly protruding belly and cupping one of her breasts in his right hand. "We could both go in a little late today, if—"

"No." Quivering, she shut her eyes tightly, knowing she had to break away from Adam, from the rich, ripe heat of his big body. "We're already taking the afternoon off for my sonogram, we can't—"

"We can do whatever we want to do." He rubbed her budded nipple through her long-sleeved cotton pullover, and nearly exploded when she moaned and threw her head back against his chest.

"Don't do this," she pleaded. "No sex. You promised."
No love. No permanent marriage. No happily ever after. No
sex! If she gave in to her desire, Blythe knew she'd wind up
getting her heart broken, and she would walk away from this
pretend marriage in love with a man who didn't love her.

Slowly, reluctantly, Adam released his hold on her. He
took a step back, separating their bodies. Still, she didn't
turn around, only stood there motionless for a few minutes, willing her wobbly legs to move.

"Don't forget to drink plenty of water before I pick you
up this afternoon," he said, his voice amazingly calm for a
man who was dying a thousand deaths at that precise moment. "Remember that Dr. Meyers said the fuller your
bladder the better. The pressure on the uterus will make the
baby more active."

"Yes, I remember. I'll be ready to leave at two o'clock.
Joy's coming in at one."

Blythe rushed out of the kitchen, snatched her purse off
the hall tree and jerked open the front door. The quicker she
got away from Adam, the better. There was only so much
temptation a woman could take. And Adam Wyatt was
temptation personified.

Blythe couldn't believe what Adam had done! Of all the
overbearing, manipulative, bossy stunts he had pulled, this
was the topper. How could she possibly be in love with a
man like him? Just when she thought he was changing, just
when he'd shown her the open-minded, understanding side
of his personality, he'd gone and done something like this.

Blythe stared at the two women who stood in front of her
work counter, both of them obviously waiting for her instructions. The older woman was probably fifty, neatly at-
tired in slacks and sweater, her blond hair draped about her
ears in a short pageboy. Martha Jean. That was her name.
But for the life of her, Blythe couldn't recall the woman's
last name.

Blythe forced a smile on her lips as she nodded at Martha Jean, then turned to the younger woman, a plump brunette with enormous brown eyes and a cute button nose. Cindy Burns.

"I'm sorry, ladies, but I really wasn't expecting you, and I'm not sure how to deal with this situation," Blythe said.

When she had arrived at Petals Plus ten minutes ago, both women had been waiting outside for her. After introducing themselves, they told her that her husband had interviewed and hired them the day before and told them to show up for work today.

Blythe was proud of the way she had thus far handled the situation. She had calmly invited the two women into Petals Plus, hung up her jacket and purse in the storeroom office and had put on a pot of decaf coffee to brew.

"We understand completely, Mrs. Wyatt," Cindy said. "Mr. Wyatt explained that this was a surprise for you, hiring us to help you around here now that you're pregnant."

"Oh, I see. Yes. Yes." Nodding her head, Blythe's forced smile made her face ache. "My husband is constantly surprising me."

"I think that's so wonderful." Martha Jean sighed dramatically. "You're so lucky to be married to Adam Wyatt. He's so handsome, so successful, so—"

"Rich," Blythe said.

"Well, yes, I'm sure he's rich, but I was going to say that he was so much in love with you. All he talked about during our interviews was you. How you worked too hard. How the Christmas season was such a busy time of year for you and that he worried you would overdo."

"He made sure we understood that you were our boss, not him," Cindy piped in. "And that he expected us to make things easier around here for you."

"Well, Cindy, Martha Jean, since I'm the boss..." She had been about to fire them both, to tell them to hit the road, that her husband's little surprise had backfired. But she looked into their eager faces, into two sets of sparkling eyes and didn't have the heart to dismiss them.

"Yes?" Cindy asked.

"Did Adam…that is, Mr. Wyatt…tell you that your jobs are only part-time and just temporary?" Blythe noted the surprised looks on their faces. "I'm sorry if he led you to believe otherwise, but I run a small business and I can't afford two full-time employees."

"Oh, my." Martha Jean giggled. "For a minute there I was worried. You needn't concern yourself with that. Mr. Wyatt said we will be on his payroll and our checks will be sent over every week by special messenger. I'm to work for you five days a week, especially every Saturday, so you can have free time to spend with your husband, and Cindy is to work part-time, to fill in when needed. Mr. Wyatt said you would let us know when our off-days will be."

So nice of Adam to leave some small decision for her to make. While her mind was still reeling with the announcement that Adam would be paying for one full-time employee and one part-time employee, the bell hanging over the inside of the front door chimed when the door opened. All three women turned to see who had entered the florist shop. Joy stopped abruptly, looking at Cindy and Martha Jean, then she glanced at Blythe, widening her eyes and arching her eyebrows in a questioning gesture.

"Please, come on in, Joy, and meet Cindy and Martha Jean. They're my two new employees. Adam hired them yesterday."

"Oh, dear me." Joy plastered a fake smile on her face when she approached the two ladies. "Nice to meet y'all."

"Well, Cindy, why don't you finish decorating the Victorian Christmas tree in the display window," Blythe said. "The ornaments are in the gold boxes in the storeroom." Cindy nodded and rushed to hunt the boxes. "And Martha Jean, you answer the telephone and handle any customers who drop in while I'm in conference with Mrs. Simpson."

"Would you like for me to check on that coffee first and get you a cup if it's ready?" Martha Jean asked.

"No, thank you. Maybe later. But feel free to help yourself." Blythe grabbed Joy by the arm and dragged her toward the small bathroom connected to the workroom.

Once inside the bathroom, Blythe closed the door, sat down on the closed commode seat and crossed her arms over her chest. "What am I going to do? I can't fire them. They're too nice, too eager, too thrilled to have a job."

"You should have already hired another part-time worker," Joy said. "You promised Adam weeks ago that you would."

"Are you taking his side?" Blythe glared up at her best friend. "After all he's done to me?"

"I'm not taking anybody's side. I'm just pointing out that if you'd kept your promise, Adam probably wouldn't have taken matters into his own hands."

"You are taking his side!"

Joy leaned over and grabbed Blythe by the shoulders. "Any other woman in the world would be thrilled to have a husband like Adam, doting on you, trying every way possible to make life easier for you."

With her mouth puckered into a childish pout, Blythe shrugged. "Don't you dare start pointing out his good points. Not now, when I'm so angry with him I could spit."

Laughing, Joy released her hold on Blythe. "He's getting to you. Admit it. Adam isn't the chest-beating Neanderthal you thought he was. And he is nothing like your stepfather. Absolutely nothing."

"No, he's nothing like Raymond." Blythe stood up. "But he isn't perfect, either. He's way too bossy. And he'll never give up hoping he can change me into Susie Homemaker."

"So what's wrong with being Susie Homemaker? That's exactly who I am, and I love it."

"There's nothing wrong with being a homemaker, in not having a career outside the home, if, like you, that's what you want. But I love my little florist shop, and someday I intend to own a nursery, too. I'd go nuts staying home all the time."

"So what do you intend to do with Adam Junior?" Joy pointed to Blythe's stomach.

"Since I'm the boss, there's no reason I can't bring the baby to work with me."

"Every day?"

"Yes, every day."

"And what if Adam Junior gets sick, what will you do then?" Joy asked.

"I'll stay home and take care of him. Of her! Dammit, Joy, will you please stop referring to my daughter as Adam Junior?"

"You're going to need full-time help after the baby comes, so why not break in your helpers now? That way they'll be able to—"

"Joy, what are you doing here?" Blythe eyed her friend suspiciously.

"Don't ask me. You're the one who dragged me into the bathroom."

"Don't play coy with me. Adam sent you over here, didn't he?" Blythe pointed her finger in Joy's face.

"I came by to get you to fix some greenery to go across my mantel." Joy smiled pleasantly. "I want small red velvet bows. No, make that plaid satin bows—"

"He knew I would be upset and he sent you over here to plead his case, didn't he?" Blythe planted her hands on her hips.

Joy slipped her arm around Blythe's shoulders. "Relax, will you? You won't be in any shape to get that sonogram done this afternoon if you stay this tense."

Blythe dropped her arms to her sides, relaxing just a bit, but she refused to look at Joy. "You honestly don't see anything wrong in what he did, do you?"

"I didn't say that. I think Adam should have discussed it with you, first, before he hired Cindy and Martha Dean—"

"Martha Jean," Blythe corrected.

"Whatever." Joy squeezed Blythe's shoulder. "But that's why he called me before he left the house. He realized he might have made a mistake. He was worried about how you would react."

"What did he think I'd do, shoot them?"

"No, I believe he was thinking more in terms of your shooting him when he comes to get you for your doctor's appointment today."

"Well, go right out there to the phone and call him and tell him that he's safe. He was right. I do need some help around here at Christmastime, and I'll really need somebody after the baby's born."

"Now you're being sensible," Joy said. "Why don't you go call him and tell him yourself."

"I can't. I don't intend to speak to him for at least a week. Maybe longer."

Shaking her head, Joy laughed and laughed, then opened the bathroom door and stepped outside. She glanced back at Blythe. "Have you ever asked yourself why Adam puts up with you?"

Adam didn't dare touch Blythe when the nurse, Helen Thrasher, showed them into the room where the sonogram would be done. He wanted to put his arm around his wife, show her his care and affection on such an important day for the two of them. But he knew when to leave well enough alone. Blythe hadn't spoken to him since he picked her up at Petals Plus. Of course, Joy had forewarned him, so he'd prepared himself for the silent treatment. Or so he thought.

"Please come in, Blythe, Adam." Dr. Meyers inclined his head toward the smiling young woman sitting across the room. "This is Whitney Lawrence, the technician who'll be in charge of your sonogram."

Nurse Thrasher handed the technician the videocassette that Blythe had brought with her so that they could have a record of the sonogram to take home with them.

"Now, Mrs. Wyatt, if you'll just lie down here, we'll get started," Whitney instructed.

"Adam, you can sit down there—" Dr. Meyers indicated a folding chair beside the examining table "—and hold Blythe's hand while you two get the first look at your son or daughter. Now, you did tell me that you want to know the sex of the child, if we can determine it, didn't you?"

"Yes," Blythe and Adam replied in unison.

Dr. Meyers smiled. "Hoping for a girl or a boy?" he asked.

"A girl," Blythe said.

"It doesn't matter," Adam said.

Whitney Lawrence lifted Blythe's blouse and lowered her skirt, exposing the rounded swell of her stomach. Adam watched in utter fascination as his wife's belly was revealed. He hadn't seen this much of Blythe since the night they made love.

"This gel will be a tad on the cool side," Whitney said as she lathered Blythe's stomach. "Using this gel will improve the conduction of the sound."

"What we're doing here today is a Level Two ultrasound. This will be a transabdominal exam," Dr. Meyers told them. "We'll be checking to see if the due date we've calculated correlates with the baby's size. This will let us know how your child is developing and if there's more than one baby."

"More than one baby?" Blythe tried to sit up, but Whitney patted her shoulders and eased her back down onto the examining table.

"This won't take more than five or ten minutes," Whitney said. "And it's totally painless."

Totally painless, huh? For whom? Blythe wondered. For someone who hadn't drunk a gallon of water? For someone who hadn't just realized she could be carrying twins? For someone who wasn't trapped in a phony marriage?

"Now, I'm going to run this transducer over your abdomen. See it?" Whitney held the object up for Blythe and

Adam's inspection. "And y'all can watch that monitor over there."

Adam sat down beside Blythe, but did not take her hand. She hadn't offered it to him, and he certainly wasn't going to just grab it. He had known there was a good chance she'd be upset when he hired two employees to work at Petals Plus without consulting her on the matter. But she kept putting off hiring any help, when she knew she needed it. He'd done the only sensible thing he could do—what any husband who wanted to take care of his wife would have done.

Blythe gasped. "Oh, look at that."

Dr. Meyers patted Blythe on the shoulder. "You can see the little heart beating, can't you?"

Blythe stared at the black-and-white images of the tiny fetus. The tiny baby. Her baby. Adam's baby.

Adam glanced at the monitor and for one split second he couldn't breathe. Dr. Meyers pointed out their child's head, arms, legs and the curve of its spine.

"Looks like we've got a thumb sucker here," Whitney Lawrence said.

"What?" Adam stared at the screen until he saw exactly what the technician meant. His child actually was sucking its thumb. "Would you look at that?"

"How precious," Blythe said. Tears misted her eyes. Happy tears. Tears she didn't even try to conceal.

She glanced at Adam and her heart skipped a beat. He stared at the monitor with a look of awe in his dark eyes. She reached out and clasped his hand. He stared down at their hands, then over at her.

"She's real, Adam. Look at her." Blythe glanced back at the monitor.

Dr. Meyers chuckled. Whitney Lawrence cleared her throat and smiled.

"What is it?" Blythe asked, her gaze moving from one person to another.

"Well, from what I can detect," Whitney said, "I wouldn't suggest rushing out to buy any frilly pink dresses."

"Look very closely, right here—" Dr. Meyers pointed to the baby's genital area "—and you can tell this baby's a boy."

"A boy?" Adam swallowed hard. A son. His son. He stared at the monitor for several seconds longer, then glanced at Blythe's shocked face.

"My baby is a boy?" Blythe asked. "Not a little girl?"

"We can't be one hundred percent certain, but in most cases we can be over ninety percent certain when we predict a boy," Dr. Meyers said. "I don't think there's too much doubt about it. Your baby is a boy."

"We're almost finished here," Whitney said. "I'll have your videotape and some black-and-white stills for y'all to take home."

Dr. Meyers grasped Adam's shoulder. "You can frame the first picture of your son and put it on your desk."

"The first picture of my son." Adam grinned. "Yeah, I suppose that's exactly what it is, isn't it?" Pictures of his son. Before birth. As a newborn. At two weeks. Two months. Two years. Images of the child flashed through Adam's mind. A plump, laughing baby with Blythe's bright hazel eyes and tufts of black hair. But then, maybe their son would have Blythe's copper hair and freckles, and his brown eyes.

He squeezed Blythe's hand. "Are you terribly disappointed? I know you were hoping for a girl."

"I'm not disappointed," she told him. "Surprised, but—" She could not erase the image of a black-eyed, black-haired little toddler holding up his plump arms to her and calling her Mama. The child was the very image of Adam.

"But what?"

"Nothing. I'll just have to start thinking of her as a him." Suddenly the baby moved. Blythe gasped loudly.

"What's wrong?" Adam gripped her hand.

"Haven't you gotten used to the baby's movements yet, Mrs. Wyatt?" Whitney asked. "I imagine he's been making his presence known for a couple of weeks now, hasn't he?"

"The baby's moving?" Adam released Blythe's hand abruptly, shot straight up out of his chair and stared down at her exposed belly. "You felt it move just then?"

"Yes," Blythe admitted, then looked at Whitney. "I felt her—him—move for the first time about ten days ago. Just a tiny little fluttering at first."

"Ten days ago," Adam muttered quietly. She had been feeling the baby move for ten damn days and she'd never said a word to him. Not one word! Why wouldn't she have told him? She had agreed that they would share everything.

Blythe and Adam left Dr. Meyers's office that day with a videotape, a stack of black-and-white stills and the image in their minds of their baby boy sucking his thumb. Adam hadn't said a word to her after he'd found out she'd kept the baby's first movements a secret from him. He couldn't help feeling hurt, left out and even a little bit betrayed.

He helped Blythe into his Lotus, then got in and drove them home. He didn't look at her or speak to her, and even though she kept stealing glances at him, she remained silent all the way to the cottage.

The minute Adam closed the front door behind him, he stared across the living room at Blythe, who stood a few feet away. She tilted her chin defiantly and met his heated glare bravely.

"I just want to know why, Blythe. Why didn't you tell me? Why didn't you share it with me?"

"Adam, I didn't tell anyone. Not even Joy."

"Joy is not that baby's father. I am! We agreed to share everything. Everything, dammit!"

"I'm sorry. I didn't realize you'd be this upset." She'd known he would resent her not having told him, but she honestly hadn't thought he'd be so furious. "I don't know if I can explain." How could she tell him that the thought of him touching her so intimately threw her into an absolute panic? Every time he touched her, no matter how innocently, she felt her body come alive, wanting and needing him to continue touching her.

"Do you dislike me that much?" he asked. "I thought we'd gotten past our misconceptions about each other. I thought we were beginning to understand each other. Was I wrong?"

"No. You weren't wrong."

"Then what's the problem? Explain it to me."

"I didn't want you to—knowing the baby was moving, you'd have wanted to—I just couldn't bear—"

"You couldn't bear for me to touch you? Is that what you're trying to say?" Adam clenched his teeth so tightly his jaw ached. His wife—the mother of his son—was telling him that she could not bear the feel of his hands on her body. A deep, raw ache sprang to life inside him, building in strength as it spread through his whole body. His muscles tensed to the point of pain. He knotted his big hands into deadly fists. "You hate my touch that much?"

"It's not what you're thinking." Blythe slipped off her coat, tossed it on the sofa and walked over to stand directly in front of Adam. "I don't hate your touch. If anything, the exact opposite is true. Don't you see? Can't you understand? That's why I can't bear for you to touch me."

He stared at her, uncertain he had understood her correctly. But then his mind began to register the meaning and he growled, the sound coming from deep in his chest. "Blythe?"

"We're in a temporary marriage of convenience. We got married because I'm pregnant, not because we were in love. In a few months, we're going to get a divorce. I just don't think I can handle a temporary sexual relationship with you."

His heart suddenly apprehended what she'd told him. That's when his body took charge, telling him that this woman—the woman who'd been tempting him for five long months now—was his for the taking.

Blythe took a step forward, grasped Adam's hand and slid it under her loose checkered blouse. His hand trembled. She felt soft and hard all at the same time, her flesh warm to the touch. He breathed in her sweet, jasmine scent.

"He doesn't move all the time, you know. It could be hours and hours before he moves again." Blythe laid her hand over Adam's.

"I don't mind spending the next few hours doing nothing but touching you," he told her.

"Adam?"

Leaving one hand on her abdomen, he reached out with the other and cupped her chin, turning her face upward. He leaned down, stared into her bright hazel eyes and kissed her. The longest, sweetest, hungriest kiss of his life.

# Eight

---

"Oh, Adam, this was what I was afraid of." Blythe placed her hands on his chest in a halfhearted attempt to shove him away.

He gripped the back of her neck, then delved his other hand beneath the stretchy waistband of her corduroy slacks and inside the top edge of her silky panties. "This is what you wanted. What we both wanted."

His voice was so husky, so totally aroused male that Blythe trembled as it reverberated around her, caressing her skin as if he'd rubbed her body with heated oil.

She wanted to deny the truth of his words, but she couldn't. She did want him, in a hungry, desperate way she'd never imagined she could want a man.

"We'll regret it later." She tried to reason with herself as well as with him. "Just like last time."

He shoved his hand between her thighs, threading his fingers through the lush curls at the junction. She gasped when he eased two fingers gently inside her, testing her readiness, assuring himself that she was as aroused as he was.

"We'll regret it if we don't." He moved his fingers in and out, stroking her core with his thumb.

Tingling heat rose from deep within her, spreading quickly, tightening her nipples and drenching her femininity. How could she resist the deep ache that racked her body?

While his fingers continued their rhythmic penetration and withdrawal, he lowered his head and kissed her again, thrusting his tongue inside her mouth, soon synchronizing both movements. Reaching up, Blythe clutched his broad shoulders for support. He walked her backward a few inches until her buttocks brushed the wall, then he hurriedly unbuttoned her blouse and reached inside her bra to encompass one swollen breast. Kneading her tender flesh, he rubbed his thumb across her peaked nipple. She cried out and he stilled his movements immediately.

"Did I hurt you?" Dear God, he'd never forgive himself if he'd caused her any pain in the fury of his passion.

"No, you—" she gasped for air "—didn't hurt me."

He began again the torturous attention to her nipple and the kernel of flesh hidden in the feminine folds of her body. Moaning deep in her throat, she closed her eyes, pressed her head back against the wall and allowed the sensations to rocket through her.

Adam felt her tightening around his fingers, felt the gush of moisture and caught her cries of completion in a tongue-thrusting kiss.

While shudders of fulfillment rippled through Blythe, he pulled her slacks and panties down her hips and legs, then unzipped his pants and freed his straining erection. He cupped her naked buttocks and lifted her up and against his throbbing sex. He thrust into her, unable to go slowly or be gentle. He had waited too long, hurt too much to be the tender lover she might want. Shivering with a rekindled sexual urgency, she panted wildly when he entered her.

"Damn, but you feel good, babe." For a few brief moments, he savored the hot, sweet ecstasy of being completely inside her, sheathed with the tight moist heat of her body. "I don't want to hurt you, but I need this—need you so much."

She locked her legs around his hips and flung her arms around his neck, burying her face in his shoulder. "You're not hurting me. Not really. You're just...just..."

"Just what?" he eased partially out of her, then grasping her hips, moved her onto him, burying himself to the hilt within her.

Sighing with intense pleasure, she gripped his shoulders, tossed her head back and smiled. "You're just filling me so completely that I'm aching from the fullness. But it's such a sweet ache."

Her confession of what it felt like to have him inside her wrapped around him like a caressing hand, hardening him to the point of agonized pleasure. And all the while the clutching rhythm of her body beckoned him to lunge deeper and harder and faster. His release hit him hard. Urging her hips into a pounding frenzy, he drained every ounce of fulfillment from his body. The hard, hammering intensity of his sex against hers flung Blythe into a deeper and more prolonged climax, the aftershocks shaking her into uncontrollable shivers.

Breathing frantically, his chest thumping, sweat drenching his flesh, Adam held Blythe, their bodies still joined. She rested her head on his shoulder while he carried her down the hall, through her bedroom and into the master bath. Standing her on her feet, he chuckled when she swayed, her knees weak. He eased her down on the vanity stool, kissed her on the nose, turned and bent down to turn on the faucets for the whirlpool tub.

Turning back to her, he slowly removed her blouse and bra. He could not resist lifting the enticing weight of her round, full breasts, now twice the size they'd been when he made love to her that night at his condo. They were enlarging with her pregnancy, preparing for the milk that would nourish their child.

Drawing in her breath and releasing it quickly several times as he caressed her, she watched him looking at her breasts and saw plainly the renewed desire in his dark eyes. Adam released her, then pulled off his pants and briefs. He was hard again. How was that possible? He'd just had the best sex of his entire life, and it hadn't been enough. It would never be enough. Not with Blythe. There was just something about her—something about the two of them together. He had always enjoyed sex, since the first time, when he was sixteen and lost his virginity to an experienced older woman—an eighteen-year-old college freshman. He'd had his share of women, but no previous experiences had prepared him for the way Blythe made him feel every time he touched her. Nor for the way he felt about her. Possessive as hell. As if he wanted to tattoo a sign on her that said Property of Adam Wyatt.

He laughed, a deep rumble in his chest. God, if he ever told her how he felt, she'd throw a fit. She would hate the very thought of him wanting to brand her with his private mark of ownership. He supposed she had every right to consider him old-fashioned. He was. He admitted it. And he couldn't help it.

He loved the way Blythe responded to him, the way she went wild in his arms. There was certainly something to be said about a strong, independent woman who knew what she wanted and gave as good as she got.

His wife was a constant source of surprises, starting with her innocence the first time they'd made love. That had been his first erroneous assumption about her. Every time he thought he had her figured out, she did the unexpected.

"Would you object if we take a long, hot soak in the tub before we go to bed?" he asked as he scooped her up into his arms.

"Is that all we're going to do? Just soak?" She wriggled against him, her hips grazing his arousal.

"For a while," he said, then stepped into the swirling water and sat, bringing Blythe down onto his lap. He eased her in front of him, between his spread legs. Her round, trim hips fit perfectly. He slipped his arms around her waist, crossing them over just beneath her breasts. She leaned back against him, resting her head on his chest.

Suddenly Blythe gasped and sat up straight. She grabbed his hand and pressed it against her belly. "He's moving, Adam. Feel him. Feel him moving inside me."

Adam held his breath when he felt his son move. Blythe held her hand over Adam's. "My God!" he said.

"I couldn't imagine what it would feel like," she said. "Joy tried to tell me, but words just can't describe how it feels."

Adam rubbed her tummy with wide, soothing strokes. "Hey, big boy, this is your father. What's the matter? Did your mama and I wake you up with all our carrying on? Are you trying to tell us to take it easy on you?"

Listening to Adam talk to her stomach, Blythe giggled. "I think he's a little young for you to be discussing the birds and bees with him."

"I didn't hurt you, did I?" Adam stilled his hand and spread out his fingers to partially cover the small melon-size swell of her abdomen. "My being so rough didn't hurt the baby, did it? I didn't mean to take you like that, babe. Honest, I didn't. It's just that once things got started, I sort of lost control."

She turned halfway around, squirming her bottom against his arousal. Twining her arms around his neck, she licked a thin, warm trail up his neck, across his jaw and stopped at his mouth.

"Don't worry so much," she told him. "I'm fine. Our son's fine. I'm young, strong, healthy and there's no reason that our having sex would harm either me or the baby."

"In that case..." Shifting Blythe's body so that she faced him, Adam surged into her with an upward lunge that took her breath away.

"Adam!" she gasped, then closed her eyes as he grabbed her by the waist, nudging her downward until she fit him like a tight glove.

*Oh, mercy me!* she thought. Just the feel of him inside her was almost enough to make Blythe lose herself. Even though Adam was her only lover, she instinctively knew that even if sex with another man might be very enjoyable, no other man could ever compare to Adam.

All her life, she had steered clear of big, old-fashioned macho guys who reminded her of her stepfather. She had always thought, when she took a lover, he would possess a gentle, artistic soul and perhaps quote poetry to her in bed. But instead, she had taken a big, strong brute as a lover—as a husband—and their lovemaking was as fierce and untamed as the wild passion inside them.

The whirlpool waters surged around their naked bodies, caressing their heated flesh with waves of swirling pleasure.

"Ride me, babe," he told her. "Ride me hard."

Their wet bodies moved in a fast, undulating rhythm, increasing in speed with each thrust, until they both exploded into earth-shattering completion simultaneously. As they trembled with release, Adam held her, kissing her with a furious need, wishing the feeling spiraling through him could last forever.

A few minutes later, he got out of the tub, then lifted her in his arms. Retrieving a couple of huge towels from the small linen closet in the bathroom, Adam threw them across Blythe and carried her into her bedroom. When he set her on her feet, the towels dropped to the floor. He picked up one and began drying her off, enjoying the sensual delight of her sweet, naked body.

"Get in bed, babe. I think we could both use a long nap before dinner," he said, then wondered if she'd think he was giving her an order. But when she smiled and turned down the covers, he dried off quickly.

She got in bed, pulled the sheet up over her breasts and watched him crawl in bed beside her. Maybe she should protest, tell him that even if they had had sex—twice—they probably shouldn't sleep together. That would make their marriage seem too real.

But when Adam reached out and took her in his arms, she forgot all about asking him to go to his own bed. She snuggled against the hard, solid wall of his big body and fell into a deep, restful sleep.

Still half-asleep the next morning, Adam caressed the bed where Blythe should have been. Not finding her, he spread his arms farther and searched for her. Groggily, he opened his eyes. Her side of the bed was empty.

"Blythe?" He listened for the sound of running water, thinking she was probably in the shower. An unusual quiet filled the air, disrupted only by the faint tick of her small, antique alarm clock.

He glanced at the clock. Six-thirty. Surely she hadn't gone to work this early, especially now that she had two extra pairs of hands around Petals Plus. Maybe she was in the kitchen whipping up a special breakfast to celebrate their night of passion. Last night, after they'd prepared and eaten dinner together, they had returned to Blythe's bed and made love again.

Adam stretched, kicking back the covers, allowing his big, long body the freedom of the entire bed. What a night they'd shared! It had been a few years since he'd made love, other than with Blythe, three times in one night. But his sexy wife kept him so horny he went around aroused all the time.

As a matter of fact, just thinking about her excited him. He wished she'd forget about breakfast, for the time being anyway, and come back to bed. He wanted her again. Right now.

"Blythe?"

No reply.

He got out of bed and strolled down the hall, stopping in the kitchen doorway. The room was empty. Not one dirty dish lay in the sink.

"Blythe?"

Naked and aroused, he prowled through the house, only to find his wife missing. He went back into her bedroom, picked up his pants off the floor and slipped into them, then went out the side door to see if Blythe's minivan was gone.

"Damn! Where has she run off to this time?" he asked himself.

The first and only other time they'd made love, he had awakened to find her gone. She had run away from him and tried to shut him out of her life because she thought their lovemaking had been a major mistake. But why would she run from him now? They were married and expecting a child and finally making progress in getting to know each other and truly understanding each other. Or so he had thought. Surely she didn't think their making love last night had been a mistake. Nothing that felt so right could possibly be wrong in any way.

Well, there was no point standing in the middle of the driveway trying to figure out why his little redheaded spitfire had fled from him. He'd just have to find her and ask her what was going on. And if she tried to shut him out this time, he'd— He'd what? Demand she come home with him where she belonged? No. Wrong strategy to use with Blythe. Reason with her? Maybe. And if all else failed, he might do a little begging. Adam grinned. Whatever it took to get her to come back home, he'd do it. Their deal had been to stay married, live together for the duration of her pregnancy and then file for a divorce only after her six-week checkup. She wasn't about to wangle out of their bargain. Not now. Not after what they shared last night.

Adam showered, shaved, dressed and downed a glass of orange juice, then hopped in his Lotus and headed toward Decatur. He made several phone calls from his car, trying to locate his wife. With the third call he struck gold. Blythe was with Joy.

"Yeah, she's here. She showed up nearly an hour ago and got us out of bed," Craig whispered. "Joy banished me to the kitchen. They're holed up in the den, probably plotting your demise."

"What do you mean, plotting my demise?" Adam clutched his cellular phone with one hand and guided the steering wheel into a U-turn with the other. He had just missed the turnoff to Joy and Craig's house.

"Well, Blythe's exact words when I opened the front door an hour ago were *Where is Joy? I've got to talk to her right now. She has to help me figure out what I'm going to do about Adam.*"

"Oh, hell. I swear, Craig, things were a lot simpler a few thousand years ago when all a man had to do was knock a woman over the head and drag her back to his cave."

Craig chuckled. "Come to the back door. I'll have a strong cup of coffee waiting for you."

Adam parked the Lotus directly behind Blythe's minivan, blocking her in, just in case she made a run for it. Following Craig's instructions, he went around to the back door and raised his hand to knock. With his crying daughter perched on his hip, Craig swung the door open.

"Come on in. Missy's throwing a fit. She woke up hungry and I'm going to have to go in there and disturb the womenfolk."

"Hey, pretty girl." Adam cuddled Missy under the chin. She stopped yelling long enough to gaze up at her godfather. Sniffling, she stuck her fist in her mouth.

"Do you understand your wife?" Adam asked his best friend.

"A little," Craig said. "But she's a woman and I'm a man, so that rules out the possibility of complete understanding on either side."

"I thought that after last night things would get better. How wrong could I be?" Adam shook his head. "Every time I make love to her, she runs. What am I supposed to make of that?"

"No way am I going to try to answer that question." Craig kissed Missy on the top of her head. "Come on, Uncle Adam. Follow us. Missy wants Mommy, and you want Aunt Blythe.''

"I don't know whether or not I want her. The woman's more trouble than she's worth.''

"I don't believe you. If she wasn't worth the trouble, you wouldn't be here." Craig leaned Missy against his chest and covered her exposed ear with his hand. "I know the look of a rutting stallion when I see one. Face it, old buddy, when you reach the point where only one woman can satisfy you, you've had it. You might as well give in.''

"What the hell are you talking about?" Adam glared at Craig. "And what are you doing covering up Missy's ears? She doesn't know what you're saying.''

"Hey, my daughter has superior intelligence. Just because she can only say Mama, doesn't mean she can't understand a lot more.''

Adam grunted, then grinned. "Let's go get this over with. I swear, if she runs, I'm going to hog-tie her.''

Craig knocked on the closed den door, and waited until Joy said, "Yes? What is it, Craig?" before he opened the door and walked in.

"Your daughter's hungry, madam.''

Joy held out her arms as she stood. "Come to Mama, sweetheart. Are you hungry?" Joy started to part her robe, then stopped abruptly when Adam stepped into the den. "Hello, Adam." Joy took Missy from Craig.

Blythe, who was sitting on the floral sofa, gasped, then jerked her head around and stared up at Adam, her eyes wide and bright and filled with a strange look. Almost like a deer caught in a car's headlights, Adam thought and suddenly realized that she was afraid. Afraid of him!

"May I speak to you alone?" Adam looked directly at Blythe.

"It's all right," Blythe told Joy. "Go on and take care of Missy. Adam and I need to talk.''

"If you need me I'll—" Joy said.

"I don't think they'll need you, honey," Craig told her.

"Right," Joy said. Craig slipped his arm around his wife's waist and led her out of the den.

"May I sit down?" Adam asked. Hell, he hated walking on eggshells, but he had no other choice. He didn't want to make a mistake by saying or doing anything that would upset or alienate Blythe. He wanted her smiling, happy and in his arms.

She nodded her acquiescence, and before she could request he not sit next to her, he plopped down on the sofa beside her. She scooted to the far edge.

Damn, he remembered how she'd done the same thing that night at his condo, during the storm. She seemed as wary of him now as she was then. But why?

"What's wrong, babe? Why'd you run away?" If only she'd look at him. But she didn't. She sat away from him, rigid and tense.

"We can't live together anymore," she said.

"What do you mean, we can't live together anymore?"

"I think it would be obvious what I mean, after what happened last night." She took a deep breath, but still refused to look at him.

"I'm afraid I don't quite understand your reasoning," he told her. "But then, of course, that's nothing new, is it?"

"We made a bargain with each other. We promised each other certain things. Last night, we broke our promise not to have sex. That changes things. Don't you see?"

"No, I don't see."

"Having sex changes our relationship, doesn't it?" She glanced at him out of the corner of her eye, then cast her gaze downward into her lap.

Was that what was bothering her? Did she think that their becoming lovers again had altered the game plan? Was she afraid he might expect her to be a real wife to him in every way, even stay married and forget the divorce?

"It doesn't have to change anything," he said cautiously, then added, "unless you want it to."

"What about you?" she asked. "Do you feel any different about our relationship now?"

What did she want him to say? God, if only he could read her mind and choose his answer accordingly. As far as he was concerned their becoming lovers again had changed their relationship—made it better, easier. Or at least, it should have. If he was totally honest with her, and with himself, he'd tell her that he wanted her now, more than ever, and that the idea of ending their relationship after their son was born didn't appeal to him in the least.

But how would she react if he was honest with her? Obviously the thought that anything between them might change on a permanent basis frightened her.

"Look, I know that making love sometimes takes on more meaning for a woman than it should." He swallowed. "Maybe you just overreacted a little to something that was bound to happen. After all, we're married, living in the same house and we're attracted to each other. It's only natural that we'd want to make love."

"Yes, I suppose it is."

He was saying what she had thought he would say, that for him, nothing had changed, while for her everything had. He wanted her for a sex partner while they were married, but he still intended to go through with the divorce once the baby was born. Their marathon of passionate lovemaking had simply been sex for him, but for her, it had been love.

After awakening this morning and mulling things over, she'd run away, hoping he'd come after her, praying that he'd rush into Joy and Craig's house and proclaim his undying, eternal love for her. Oh, brother, had she been a fool. Adam might desire her sexually, but he'd never accept her as she was for his life's partner. She just wasn't what he wanted.

And is he what you really want? she asked herself. Married to Adam, you could never be sure if, in wanting to please him and make him happy, you wouldn't give up a little more of yourself every day. Could you trust yourself not to change, not to try to be more the kind of wife he expects, instead of the kind of woman you are?

He reached out and ran the back of his hand along her cheek. Sucking in a deep breath, she closed her eyes, savoring the feel of his flesh against hers.

"We made a bargain," he said. "One that we both intend to keep, except for the not having sex clause." He grinned. "That one didn't make much sense anyway, considering how attracted we are to each other."

Blythe opened her eyes, clasped his hand and removed it from her face. "Let me get this straight. Our being lovers didn't change anything as far as our original agreement is concerned."

"That's right." Liar, his conscience screamed.

"And you want us to continue being lovers, since we can't seem to resist each other?"

"Why should we fight the attraction? I want you. You want me. What's the harm in our enjoying a sexual relationship while we're married?"

"And after our divorce, we'll both be free to find other... sexual... partners. Right?" she asked.

No! Hell, no! He'd kill any man who touched her. She was his, and his alone. "Yeah. Sure. After the divorce," he said.

"I'm not sure if I can agree to—to continue having sex with you."

He took both of her hands into his and held them between their bodies. "Come home with me now, and promise me that no matter what, you won't run away again. And I promise that we'll play this thing by ear and let whatever happens, happen."

"What do you mean by that?"

"I mean that I won't take for granted that we'll continue having sex, but that if and when we find ourselves wanting each other and do make love, there won't be any recriminations or placing blame afterward. Can you agree to that?"

Blythe considered her options. She could leave Adam. She could stay with him and refuse to have sex. Or she could stay with him and allow herself the pleasure of having him for her lover—until their divorce.

"I'll come home," she said. "After work today. But I want a couple of days to let the dust settle, to let all that steam we created cool off before I agree to anything. Just give me some space. And don't touch me. I can't think straight when you touch me."

"I know the feeling, babe." Only too well. When he touched her, he lost all sense of reason. If she had any idea the extent of the power she wielded over him, she could destroy him. "Friends again, and maybe, sometimes, lovers?" He held out his hand.

Trying to smile, she finally forced a weak little grin. "Friends again? Yes. Lovers? Maybe."

She didn't touch his hand. She didn't dare.

# Nine

Adam checked his watch again. Hell, he had to stop doing that. All morning he'd been acting like a worm in hot ashes, counting the minutes until Blythe showed up for their lunch date. Since their agreement four days ago to give themselves a little time to cool off, things had returned to normal. Normal, if you called sleeping in separate beds and being careful to not touch each other normal.

His months of celibacy had ended when he had spent one night feasting on the richness of Blythe's body, only to find out the next morning that he might be forced to go back on a starvation diet for another five or six months!

He could find it easy to hate Blythe, to accuse her of trying to torment him by withholding sex, if he didn't know she was hurting as much as he was. He could see it in her eyes whenever she looked at him. She wanted him. She wanted what they'd had together, but for her own illogical reasons she was denying them both the earth-shattering pleasure they found in making love.

Today he intended to change things. He wasn't going to push too hard and make her balk. He would take things slow and easy—just not too slow. He wanted his wife naked and aroused and lying beneath him before the night ended. He wanted to hear her crying out, begging for more, as she wrapped herself around him and trembled with release.

He had made up his mind, and nothing was going to stop him. He couldn't spend the next half a year celibate, and he didn't want any other woman. So that left him with only one sensible thing to do. Adam was going to seduce his wife.

He had thought she might refuse his invitation to lunch and a shopping trip afterward, and he'd had a backup plan in mind. But she had agreed quickly, especially to the shopping trip, admitting she needed some maternity clothes and that it wouldn't be a bad idea to choose some things for the nursery.

A tightfisted knot of pain formed in his stomach at the thought of Blythe taking their son and moving out of the house. She'd asked him if he didn't think it was a waste of time and money to go to the trouble of decorating a nursery in the house they shared, since the baby would only be there for a short time. Even if Blythe and their son were going to move into a new house after their divorce, Adam wanted Blythe and him to decorate a nursery together now. He had insisted on the nursery. He was always insisting on some issue or another.

Sometimes he knew he pushed her too hard, trying to take care of her, doing what he thought was best. And heaven help him, he couldn't stop doing the very things that drove her crazy. He was an aggressive, take-charge kind of man, but that didn't mean he wasn't willing to see Blythe's side of things, wasn't willing to meet her halfway.

He was trying, dammit. He was trying hard. And he had to admit, so was she. Neither of them was used to living with someone else, to sharing their lives with someone else, to having to constantly consider another person's feelings.

"You can't go in there!" Sandra Pennington's voice rang out loud and clear.

Adam jerked his head around to see the door to his office swing open. Angela Wright, encased in tight jeans and a fox fur jacket, flew into the room, Adam's secretary on her heels.

"I'm sorry, Mr. Wyatt," Sandra said. "I told Ms. Wright you couldn't be disturbed, but, as you can see, she didn't listen."

"Adam, darling, tell this woman to go away." Angela unzipped her jacket, revealing the body-hugging turtleneck that accentuated the swell of her huge breasts. "I knew you'd want to see me, no matter how busy you are."

"Thanks for trying, Sandra," Adam said. "I can handle things."

Frowning, Sandra eyed the intruder, a look of disapproval on her face. "Don't forget your lunch date in about fifteen minutes."

"I haven't forgotten. If my date shows up before Ms. Wright leaves, please entertain her in your office."

"You really shouldn't keep your date waiting, Mr. Wyatt." Sandra gave him a warning stare.

"I don't intend to," Adam assured her. "Now, go back to work. I can take care of this problem."

Sandra gave him a yeah-sure look, shrugged and exited his office.

Angela tossed her jacket into a nearby chair, then turned and smiled at Adam. "Who's your lunch date? Someone the little wifey doesn't know about, I'll bet." When Adam didn't reply, Angela slinked across the room, rounded his desk and leaned over the back of his chair to drape her arms around his neck. "If you'd wanted a long, hot lunch—" she flicked Adam's ear with the tip of her tongue "—all you had to do was call me."

Adam flung off her clinging arms, shot up out of his chair and glared at his former girlfriend. "I'm having a long, hot *lunch* with the woman of my choice."

"I guess I'm too late, huh? It didn't take you as long as I thought to go looking for a little action on the side." Angela swayed her hips provocatively as she sauntered closer. "I figured you'd be wanting someone more exciting than that freckle-faced, big-eyed wife of yours. How far along is she? Enough for her tummy to be getting in the way?"

Adam laughed. "Not long after we started our affair, I realized I didn't like you very much, Angela. That I didn't want to date you anymore. But I never knew what a real bitch you are."

Angela laid her hands on Adam's chest. "You seemed to like me well enough when we were making love."

"We had sex, Angela. A woman like you doesn't make love, she makes conquests."

She rubbed herself intimately against him, then slid her arms around his neck. She tried to kiss him—he turned his head to avoid the kiss. She squirmed against him again. "What's the matter with you? Has the little wifey emasculated you?"

"I don't want *you,*" Adam said. "That should be plain enough for even you to understand." He grabbed her shoulders. She flung her arms around his waist. "I have a wife," he told her. "I don't need or want a mistress."

"If you're so satisfied being stuck with your pregnant wife, why are you entertaining another woman for lunch today, darling? I'm just sorry you didn't choose me. But no hard feelings. Call me next time you need somebody to scratch that big, bad itch of yours. Now, give me a good-bye kiss and I'll be on my way."

"No kiss," Adam told her.

"Just a teeny-weeny little kiss?" She puckered up her lips and inclined her head toward his.

At that precise moment, with Adam clutching Angela's shoulders and Angela's mouth a whisper from his, the office door swung open. Adam saw Blythe standing in the doorway, Sandra Pennington trying desperately to block her path.

"I'm sorry, Mr. Wyatt, but Mrs. Wyatt wouldn't wait."

Adam flung Angela away from him, took a tentative step toward Blythe and stopped dead in his tracks. The expression on his wife's face would have stopped a battalion of trained soldiers.

"This is not what it looks like," Adam said.

"Of course it's not." Angela glided across the room, picked up her fur jacket, tossed it over her shoulder and smiled at Blythe. "He was just kicking me out. He said he didn't have time for me today since he had a hot lunch date with another woman." Angela turned to Adam, blew him a kiss and slinked past Blythe and Sandra.

"Don't overreact," Adam said. "Please let me explain before you make a judgment call on what you think you walked in on."

Blythe didn't move, didn't speak, didn't blink. Adam wasn't sure she even breathed.

He took several more slow, cautious steps toward her. "Today is the first time I've seen her since she showed up, uninvited, to our wedding reception. And she came here, today, uninvited."

Blythe knotted her hands into fists. Her nostrils flared. She narrowed her eyes to two glaring, golden green slits. "She might not have been invited," Blythe said. "But obviously she wasn't unwelcome."

"That's not true. I told her to leave. She wanted a good-bye kiss before she—"

Adam ducked just in time as Blythe's handbag came sailing through the air, missing his head by mere inches.

She reached out, grabbed a handful of magazines off a table near the door and tossed them at him, then she lifted a pair of small glass sculptures off the table and flung them, one at a time. The first sculpture hit the side of Adam's desk, cracking the glass surface. The second hit Adam square in the stomach. He grunted and grabbed his belly.

"You promised me that you wouldn't...wouldn't... I should have known you didn't stay celibate all these months," Blythe screamed. "You were lying to me all along, seeing that woman behind my back. You're nothing but a lying, cheating, no-good—man!"

Adam stalked across the room. Blythe backed out into Sandra's office.

"I haven't had sex with another woman since the first time I made love to you, and you damn well know it."

Adam kept walking toward her. She kept backing up. Sandra stood beside her desk, glancing back and forth between her boss and his wife.

"I don't believe you. You had your arms around that woman. You were going to kiss her!"

"I was trying to shove her off me! And *she* was trying to kiss *me!*"

"Do you honestly expect me to believe you?" Blythe shook her index finger at Adam and blinked away her angry tears.

Before he could reply, she turned around and stormed out of the Wyatt Construction Company's offices, hurried down the hall and punched the elevator Down button. The moment the elevator doors parted, she rushed in and hit the One button for the first floor.

Adam reached the elevator just as the doors began to close. He stuck his foot between the doors and grabbed each side, pressing the doors apart.

When he stepped into the elevator, Blythe retreated to the corner and crossed her arms over her chest. She glared at him, but had to force herself not to laugh. He looked ridiculous standing there, his face red with anger and his black eyes glowering—with her purse hanging over his shoulder.

He followed her line of vision, grunted, slid her purse off his shoulder and held it out to her. "You forgot this."

Her lips twitched, but she managed to contain her smile. Accepting her purse, she nodded.

"You asked me if I expected you to believe me." He moved in closer, hovering over her, as the elevator began its descent. "Well, the answer is yes, I do, especially since I'm telling the truth."

"Hmph . . . I'll bet."

"I have not been fooling around with Angela." Exasperated, Adam threw up his hands. "I don't even like the woman."

"You don't have to like someone to . . . to . . ."

"No, but you do have to want them." Adam closed in on Blythe, placing his hands on each side of the elevator wall behind her. "And there's only one woman I want."

Blythe swallowed. Her face flushed. Heat suffused her whole body.

He certainly sounded convincing. She wanted to believe him. Needed to believe him. Dammit, she *did* believe him. But she had no intention of letting him off the hook so easily. Maybe he hadn't been having an affair with that bleached-blond bimbo, but he'd been touching her, had been practically kissing her when Blythe had walked into his office.

Adam had said that Angela was trying to kiss him. Blythe tried to recall the the scene she'd barged in on, focusing on every detail, especially Angela Wright's pouty red mouth all puckered up for Adam's kiss.

The elevator stopped on the first floor and the doors parted. Blythe slid under his arm, leaving Adam alone in the elevator. He caught up with her just outside the building, his long legs taking two steps for her every one.

He grabbed her by the arm. "Let's go out for lunch and talk this over."

"I'm not going anywhere with you!" She jerked away from him and hurried out into the parking lot.

"Oh, yes, you are!" Adam shouted as he raced up behind her, lifted her off her feet and into his arms.

"Put me down!" Although wiggling and squirming with agitation, she grabbed him around the neck. "I hate your doing this, you know. Just because you're bigger and stronger, you think you can make me do whatever you want!''

Adam paid no heed to his wife's tirade or the curious stares of people in the parking lot as he carried Blythe to his car. He unlocked the door, dumped her into the passenger seat, secured her safety belt and locked her in. By the time he got in on the other side, she had unbelted herself and was trying to open the door. Adam reached across the seat, grabbed both her hands in one of his and locked her safety belt in place with the other.

''We're going out for lunch, then I'm taking you shopping,'' he told her.

''I don't want to go anywhere with you.''

''Well, that's too bad because we're going. I don't intend to let Angela ruin our plans. I've been looking forward to spending a few hours with my wife.''

''Don't I have anything to say about what I want?''

''You wanted to have lunch with me and go shopping for maternity clothes before you found Angela in my office.'' Adam revved the motor, then backed the car out of the parking lot.

Blythe crossed her arms over her chest, suddenly feeling very unattractive. She'd always been petite, small-boned, small-breasted and cursed with a thatch of unruly auburn hair, a freckled nose and eyes way too big for her little face. Compared to the Amazonian proportions of Angela's voluptuous body, Blythe decided she probably looked like a kid. ''She's very sexy, isn't she?''

''Who?''

''Angela, dammit. Who have we been arguing about?''

''Yes, Angela is very sexy,'' Adam said. ''If you like the type.''

''You liked the *type*, didn't you? You dated her for months. You slept with her.'' Blythe wished the thought of Adam making love to another woman—any other woman, but Angela in particular—didn't bother her so much. But it did. How in the world would she handle things after their divorce? There were bound to be other women in his life, in his bed. Dear Lord, what if he married again?

"I thought Angela was my type." Adam shrugged. "I was wrong." He glanced at Blythe. She looked back at him. "Besides, my taste in women has changed. None of the women I used to date would be my type now."

Adam kept his vision focused on the road. Blythe breathed in a deep, calming breath. She had made a total fool of herself acting like a jealous wife, which of course was exactly what she was. But if she couldn't learn to control her emotions, Adam might figure out the truth. He might realize she was in love with him. And that would never do.

"She offered to have sex with you, didn't she?" Blythe asked.

"I turned down her offer."

"Why?"

"Why do you think?"

"Because you promised me that you wouldn't have sex with anyone else while we were married," Blythe said. If she had learned one thing about Adam over the last few months, it was that he was a man of his word. That's the reason she believed him, the reason she trusted him.

"And..." Adam cut his eyes in Blythe's direction.

"And what?"

"That wasn't the only reason I turned her down," Adam said.

"I know you said that she isn't your type anymore. Right?"

Adam veered off the main road and into the parking lot of a minimall, whipped into a parking space and killed the engine.

"I thought we were having lunch at the Italian Garden," Blythe said. "Why are you stopping here?"

Adam leaned over and grasped Blythe's face in both his hands. "You know what my type is now, Mrs. Wyatt? My type is a petite redhead, with a sassy mouth, an independent streak in her a mile wide, who likes to watch old horror movies and baseball games on TV with me, who is jealous of all my old girlfriends, and who makes me hard every time she looks at me with her big hazel eyes."

"Adam!"

He kissed her on the nose, then lifted her hand and rubbed it over his crotch. "All you have to do is look at me and I want you, babe. You. Only you."

"I don't know why I should believe you, but I do." She snatched her hand away, then lifted it to touch his cheek.

"You know I won't lie to you," he said. "Our marriage may not be real and we might not have been in love when we made our vows, but as long as you're my wife, you'll be my only woman."

She wasn't going to apologize or admit that she had overreacted to finding Angela in his office. Nor was she going to admit how much his promise of fidelity meant to her. But she did owe him some measure of concession. It was up to her to offer an olive branch and help return their relationship to its former friendly—very friendly—terms.

"Adam?"

"What?"

"You know I have to work late tonight."

"Yes."

"You could come over to the shop and help me. I could tell Martha Jean she won't have to work tonight, and you and I could discuss how we want to decorate the nursery, and we could order pizza, and—"

"Is this your way of saying you're sorry you misjudged me?" he asked.

Sighing she unsnapped her seat belt, cupped his face with her hand, leaned over and kissed him, then retreated quickly. "It's my way of saying that I approve of your new taste in women."

"If you don't stop looking at me that way, I'm going to take you right here, right now." He growled the words, but his eyes were smiling.

She caressed his chest, then ran her hand down his stomach and boldly fondled his arousal. Adam groaned. "I know a better way for me to say I'm sorry." She lifted her hand, redid her seat belt and sat up straight. "Tonight."

With her greatest fear a reality—falling in love with Adam—she really didn't have a logical reason to keep him at arm's length. Even if he couldn't be hers forever, she could make him hers for a little while.

Adam's body grew harder. His mind reeled with anticipation. Tonight, he thought, and smiled.

"Here. That's the last one." Adam tossed Blythe the red velvet bow, then stretched his back, lifting his hips up off the stool where he sat beside his wife at her work desk. "Now, I'm ready to devour that pizza."

Blythe slid off her stool, grunting when her feet hit the floor. Every muscle in her body ached. She and Adam had been working for over three hours preparing a huge order of Christmas wreaths for a local church that wanted one for every church door, inside and out.

"Let me give you a back rub, babe." He stood, grasped her shoulders and smiled when she sighed. "I had no idea your job was so tiring." He massaged her shoulders. "To be honest, I guess I don't know very much about being a florist. I thought all you did was arrange and deliver flowers."

"That was the florist of yesterday," Blythe said, flexing her back as Adam moved his hands downward, pressing and kneading her sore, tired muscles. "Not only do I arrange and deliver flowers, I have a whole selection of silk flowers and make arrangements for people's homes. And I sell all sorts of accessories for the home and garden."

"Do you really want to expand your business to include a nursery?" Adam asked, sliding his hand under the new hunter green maternity top they'd bought on their shopping spree this afternoon. His hand stilled on her soft, warm flesh.

She sighed. "Don't stop. It feels so good. And yes, after the baby's a little older, I'd like to buy some property and combine my florist shop with a nursery."

"Would you consider letting me buy the land for you?" He continued massaging her shoulders and back.

"No, I wouldn't. You'll be doing enough for me after...after our divorce. Building me and the baby a house and paying the salaries of my two employees and—"

"I'm a rich man, babe. Most women in your situation would take advantage of that fact."

Tilting her head to one side she looked up at him without turning completely around. "I'm not most women."

Before she knew what was happening, he turned her around, lowered his head and kissed her. She jerked away from him.

"What was that for?" she asked.

"That's for being you, and not most women."

"Oh." Blythe smiled. "I'll accept that answer. I liked it. You can rub my back some more. I like that, too."

Chuckling, Adam pulled her back against him, slipped his arm around her waist and drew her hips into the cleft between his slightly parted legs. "This is what feels good." He moved against her, letting her feel his rigid sex.

"Pizza time." She pulled out of his embrace and practically ran into the back storeroom where Adam had laid their pizza ten minutes ago when the delivery boy arrived earlier than expected.

Adam followed her. "No use running, babe. It won't do any good. If I thought running would cool my blood, I'd run clean out of the country."

"I'm not running," she lied, but kept her back to him so he couldn't see her face. "I'm just hungry. As a matter of fact, I'm starving." She patted her tummy. "And so is Elliott."

"Elliott?"

Blythe turned slowly and smiled at Adam. "Would you mind terribly if we name him Elliott? I was an only child and my father's name died with him."

"I don't know, babe. Elliott sounds so...so..."

"So what?"

"So prissy."

"It does not! It sounds distinguished and sophisticated."

"Elliott, huh?"

"Elliott Adam Wyatt," she suggested.

A warm satisfied feeling spread through Adam when she spoke the name she had chosen for their child. Her father's name. And his name.

"If Elliott Adam Wyatt is hungry, then we'd better feed him," Adam said. "Do we have paper plates? Some napkins? Something to drink?"

"I have a feeling that if Elliott takes after his father, I'll spend the whole first year of his life doing nothing but feeding him and changing his diaper."

"I can't do much to help with the feeding, until he starts eating baby food, but I can change a diaper, if you'll show me how."

She wanted to ask Adam if he was going to be around often enough to take on diaper duty, but she didn't want to spoil the moment.

She reached under a counter and pulled out a sack of plastic cups, utensils and paper plates. "I'll take care of this," she told him. "You get us some colas out of the refrigerator over there." She pointed at a minirefrigerator, not much bigger than an ice chest, which had been placed in the corner near a row of coolers containing an array of colorful flowers.

"You're not supposed to be drinking colas," Adam said. "Caffeine isn't good for Elliott."

"I can drink the decaf kind," she told him.

He retrieved two cans from the fridge, making sure Blythe's contained a decaffeinated drink, then popped the lids and set the colas on the small round table where she had placed their slices of pepperoni, black olive and mushroom pizza. They'd both been surprised to learn they liked their pizza the same way.

She chatted away about this and that, mostly about the weeks and months ahead until the baby's birth. Part of the time he actually heard what she was saying and took part in the conversation. The rest of the time, he watched her talk and eat and laugh, and wondered how it was possible that just looking at her turned him inside out. What was it about Blythe that made her so irresistible?

He cleaned up after they ate, tossing everything into a plastic trash bag. Blythe protested that she could wash the utensils and cups for reuse.

"Why the hell would you use disposable stuff and then wash it for reuse?" he asked.

"Because I'm thrifty," she replied.

"I'll buy you some new plastic cups, forks and spoons," he told her. "I'm throwing these away."

"Suit yourself. I've got to repot a couple of Christmas cactus that Cindy accidentally knocked off their display shelf earlier."

"If you'll show me what to do, I'll help you." He dropped the garbage bag by the back exit, then turned and followed her out to her work counter.

"You can get that bag of potting soil—" she pointed under the work counter "—and lift it up here." She patted the wide wooden top.

He followed her instructions, then sat down on the stool beside her. "What now?"

"Are you sure you want to do this? It'll mean getting your hands all dirty."

Blythe eyed Adam's immaculate white shirt, and wondered just how long it had been since CEO Adam Wyatt had played in the dirt. As long as she had known him, he'd been perfectly groomed, often wearing a suit and tie.

She stuck her hand into the bag of potting soil and pulled out a clump of dark, rich dirt.

"Just because I'm the boss of Wyatt Construction doesn't mean I don't still get my hands dirty occasionally." He watched her packing the dirt in her fist and wondered what she was doing. He could tell by the look in her eyes that she was up to something. "When I was a kid, I worked alongside my father's employees, doing the hard, backbreaking work. I wasn't afraid of a little dirt then, and I'm not now."

"Are you sure?" she asked, her tone playful. Drawing back her hand, she aimed and threw the clump of potting soil at Adam.

The dirt hit him on the chest, the clump falling apart upon impact. Particles flew upward and caught in his chest hair exposed by his unbuttoned collar; the rest fell down the front of his white shirt.

"Want to play, huh?" He eased off his stool.

Blythe jumped off her stool and ran around to the other side of the work counter. "Do you realize I've never seen you dirty?"

"Is that right?" Adam reached inside the bag and pulled out a handful of soil. "Come to think of it, I've never seen you dirty, either."

"Stop and think about what you're doing," she cautioned as she began backing away from him. "I'm a pregnant lady."

"Yeah, I know." He rounded the edge of the wooden counter. "You're a playful pregnant lady."

"Now, Adam—"

He tossed the dirt ball, hitting his target—her shoulder. Dirt flew across her neck and up into her hair. Sputtering, she shook her head, then dashed toward the open bag sitting on the countertop. Before Adam could grab her, she snatched up another handful of dirt and threw it, hitting him on the side of his head.

"Babe, I guess you know this is war." He picked up the bag and headed directly toward Blythe. "Ever had a dirt bath?"

Squealing, she ran into the back storage room and tried to close the door, but Adam was too quick. He grabbed her, jerked her up against him, then lifted the sack of dirt over their heads and turned it upside down. Three-fourths of the soil cascaded over Blythe; a fourth of it covered Adam.

He dropped the empty sack to the floor and looked at Blythe, her face streaked with dirt stains. She was looking up at him and laughing. He pulled her into his arms.

"Did you know that you're beautiful when you're dirty, Mrs. Wyatt?"

"So are you, Mr. Wyatt." She lifted her arms and slid them around his neck. "Why'd you shower us with the whole bag of dirt?"

"I thought if we got dirty enough, we might have to go home and play in the whirlpool bath together."

She wriggled against him. "Yeah? Well, what would you say if I told you I'd rather stay here and play in the dirt with you?"

"Babe, you'd better not be tempting a guy unless you're serious."

Blythe glanced out into the florist shop at the work counter behind the screened partition. "I've heard that people can make love just about anywhere, under any conditions."

Adam took her mouth in a kiss that left her breathless. She clutched his shoulders when he lifted her off her feet, then wrapped her legs around his hips. Cupping her buttocks, he walked out of the storage room and directly to the work counter. Without breaking the kiss, he deposited her on top of the counter and unzipped her green knit maternity top.

In her haste to undo his shirt, she popped several buttons. He raised her arms and pulled her top over her head, then took off his open shirt and threw it on the floor. He kissed the swell of both breasts while he unhooked her bra. She unbuckled his belt and undid his slacks.

Blythe wanted him. Here. Now. Like this. She ran her hands over his chest, stopping to torment his tiny nipples. Adam groaned, then lifted her up and jerked her knit maternity slacks and lace panties down to her knees. Grunting, panting, groping, they undressed and came together in a wild, raw fury. Adam surged into her with a fierce hunger, his desire too strong to temper it with gentleness. She responded with an equal passion, taking him as surely as he took her. Nothing mattered to either of them except the hot, demanding need that drove them harder and harder until the world shattered around them and shook them to the very depths of their souls.

Later—much later—Blythe lay awake in her bed at the cottage, Adam asleep at her side. Here she was in a no-win situation, in love with a man who had married her for one reason and one reason only. She had snared him in the tender trap.

Blythe cried silently, afraid of what the future held for her and Adam—and little Elliott.

# Ten

---

Adam took one last look at the blueprints for Blythe's house, then folded them and slipped them into the cardboard tube. He'd take them home to her tonight so she could make any changes she wanted. Tomorrow he'd drop them by the architect and have him incorporate Blythe's suggestions into the plans.

The plans for her dream house. The house he had promised to build her. The house where she and their son would live after the divorce.

When he had married Blythe, he had thought of their divorce as nothing more than part of their bargain. Now he found himself plotting ways to postpone the end of their marriage. Maybe he could renegotiate terms, persuade Blythe to wait until Elliott Adam Wyatt's first birthday before going through with the divorce. After all, the first year of their son's life was crucial—to the child and to them. In that first year, Adam and Blythe could bond with the baby and surround him with constant love and attention.

He had agreed to let her keep the child with her that first year, but he hated the idea of living separately from them. He would miss so many of his son's *firsts* if he wasn't with him every day.

He had hinted to Blythe several times over the past few weeks, ever since they had actually begun to live as man and wife, that he wasn't in any hurry to end their marriage. But whether she had simply not picked up on his subtle hints or had chosen to ignore them, she had made no reference to their divorce.

He knew that a divorce was inevitable. Even though they had become friends, discovering they had quite a lot in common and could compromise whenever they disagreed—at least on most subjects—they were still the same two people they were when they'd married. He was still an old-fashioned guy who couldn't change his macho stripes overnight. Hell, he doubted he would ever be able to stop trying to take care of his wife—and that was the one thing Blythe hated most. She often saw his attempts to take care of her, to make life easier for her, as his way of trying to dominate and control her. God knew, he didn't mean it that way.

He had come to realize that a woman didn't have to be the perfect homemaker in order to be a good wife and mother. And there was something to be said in favor of a strong, independent woman with whom he could discuss business-related problems and know she would not only understand but often help him come up with solutions. Then of course, there was the incredible sex. He and Blythe couldn't touch each other without catching fire.

He had grown accustomed to her sleeping in his arms every night. He liked knowing she was there. Safe and secure. Of course they still argued, more often than not over silly things, or at least things that seemed silly in retrospect. She had finally forgiven him for hiring two employees for Petals Plus without her permission, but she warned him that she would never allow him to get away with something so underhanded again. He tried to rein in his protective, controlling tendencies as much as possible, but asking him not to try to take care of her and their child was like asking him not to breathe.

And the crazy thing was he knew that a divorce wouldn't change how he felt. As far as he was concerned, Blythe and Elliott would always belong to him. Even if she married someone else. Adam plunged his closed fists down atop his desk, tossed his head back and growled, the sound dark, furious and agonized.

Blythe placed the Noah's Ark lamp on top of the white chest of drawers, stepped back and smiled when she saw how perfect it looked. Turning slowly around and around, she hugged herself as she viewed the nursery from every angle. In the past seven weeks she and Adam had turned this third bedroom into a special world for Elliott. She had chosen pale pastel shades of blue, pink, yellow and green to accent the white furniture and had chosen to use the currently popular Noah's Ark theme for the entire room. Naturally, Adam had spared no expense, and she had finally stopped reminding him that by the time Elliott was two months old, they would be divorced and she and the baby moved into another house.

Adam didn't seem inclined to discuss dissolving their marriage, and she knew the reason why. Elliott. Adam couldn't bear the thought of being separated from his son. But how could she stay married to a man who only wanted to keep her in his life because she and his child were a package deal? Besides, even though she and Adam had become friends as well as lovers, he still infuriated her sometimes when he made decisions for her. She had to admit that he didn't do it often—but he still did it!

Maybe, if he loved her, she could learn to overlook his macho faults, since he truly was trying to do better. But he didn't love her. The word had never been mentioned. He wanted her, or at least he had up to now. Every night she wondered if this would be the last night—the last time he made love to her. Surely he couldn't find her desirable. Not now. She had once laughed when she'd told him she would eventually look like a Volkswagen Beetle, but now that she was round as a butterball, the thought made her cry.

He'd made slow, sweet love to her last night, eliciting cries of pleasure. She loved the way he made love to her, and had become addicted to being touched by him. What would she do when he no longer wanted her, when the sight of her fat, ugly body repulsed him?

Blythe swallowed down the tears nudging against her throat. Checking her watch, she realized how late it was and decided she'd take a nice warm shower before Adam came home. She had left work early today, leaving Petals Plus in Martha Jean's capable hands. Now that the Christmas holiday season was over and Valentine's Day was still a couple of weeks away, business had slowed down considerably.

She walked down the hall, through her bedroom and into the master bath. Undressing slowly, she examined her body. Her breasts were swollen and very sensitive. Her stomach was huge. Of course, she was almost seven months pregnant and Elliott was growing by leaps and bounds.

She caressed her tummy. Her son kicked. She could see the outline of his little foot pressing against her abdomen. "Hello, Elliott. Mommy's feeling sorry for herself today. Daddy's bringing home the plans for our new house, the house you and I are going to live in when Daddy and I get a divorce."

When tears filled her eyes, she wiped them away. "And when you're a year old, you'll live with Daddy part of the time. I won't like not having you with me all the time, but I won't ever let you know how I feel."

She finished undressing, turned on the shower and stepped inside. The warm water felt heavenly. She tossed back her head and let the spray hit her in the face and on her neck.

As she lathered her body, she rubbed her belly and continued talking to her unborn child. "Your daddy's a pretty nice man, you know? There was a time when I thought he was nothing but a ruthless, aggressive macho jerk. But that was before I really got to know him.

"Oh, he's not perfect. Sometimes he makes me so angry I could strangle him. He just can't get it through his head that I'm capable of taking care of myself without any help from him.

"And I know that he still wishes I'd change into some 1950s TV sitcom mom, who'd stay home and bake cookies all day long." She patted her tummy. "I'll bake cookies for you, don't you worry. But I'm not going to stay home. I'll take you with me to Petals Plus every day. You'll like it there, surrounded by flowers. And in a few years, when you're old enough to start kindergarten, I'm going to expand my business and start that nursery I've always wanted. And you'll be there with me after school and in the summers, and...." Tears streamed down her face.

Blythe stayed in the shower until the skin on her toes and fingers puckered and she had discussed all her confused emotions with her son. By the time she dried off and slipped into her robe, she was crying so hard that everything around her became a teary blur.

Adam opened the front door, the house plans tucked under his arm. "Blythe? Hey, babe, where are you?"

He didn't smell supper cooking, so she wasn't in the kitchen. No big deal. He'd order takeout later, and they could snuggle in front of the fire.

"Blythe?" He laid the tube containing the house plans on the dining room table, then headed down the hall. He glanced in the nursery, thinking she might be sitting in the white rocker where she often enjoyed resting when she came in from the florist shop.

When he entered their bedroom—and that's how he thought of it now, as their bedroom—he removed his jacket and tie and tossed them on the bed.

"Blythe?" Where was she? He knew she was home. Her minivan was in the garage.

He opened the door to the bathroom and found her sitting on the vanity stool, trembling as she sobbed. He rushed over to her, knelt on one knee and put his arms around her. She looked at him, her face wet with tears, her eyes red and swollen.

"Babe, what's wrong? Are you sick? Is it the baby? Is—"

"Elliott is fine. And—" Sob. Sob. "—I'm not sick." Sob. Sob.

"Something's wrong. What is it? Tell me? A problem at work?"

She wiped her face with the back of her hand, sucked in a deep breath, let it out and glared at Adam. "You're not supposed to be home yet."

"I left early," he told her. "I brought the house plans. I knew you'd want to go over them as soon as I got them. You're going to love this house. It's everything you said you wanted."

Suddenly she burst into a fresh round of tears. Adam rubbed his hands up and down her arms, trying to soothe her. She squirmed on the vanity seat, cried even harder and turned her head away from him.

"Blythe, you're scaring me. Can't you tell me what's wrong?"

Shaking her head negatively, she crossed her arms over her protruding stomach and hugged herself tightly.

"Come on, babe. You know I'll fix it, or at least try to," Adam said. "Just tell me what I can do to make things all right."

When he tried to kiss her, she shrieked and shoved him away. Adam's butt landed on the floor. Blythe jumped up off the vanity stool and ran out of the bathroom. He sat on the floor several minutes, trying to figure out exactly what had happened. For at least the hundredth time since he'd married Blythe, he thought about how he didn't understand women, his wife in particular. The doctor had explained to him, Joy had cautioned him and Craig had warned him about how emotional and moody a pregnant woman could be. But Blythe had to take top honors. This stunt today totally baffled him.

When he got up and walked into their bedroom, he found her sitting in the middle of the bed, huddled in a ball, her feet tucked up under her and her arms wrapped around her stomach.

He sat down beside her and smiled. She glared at him. Okay, so smiling was the wrong approach. He frowned. She glared even harder. He winked at her.

"Are you making fun of me?" she asked, her voice edged with the residue of her tears.

He reached for her, but she leaned away from him. He let his hand drop to his side. "I'd never make fun of you, babe."

"I guess I'm pretty funny-looking, aren't I? I'm fat as a pig. No, I'm fat as a hog. And my face is as round as a balloon, and my fingers are so swollen I can hardly slip my rings on and off, and…I'm just huge and ugly and…" The tears started again. Filling her eyes. Trickling down her cheeks.

So that was the problem, Adam thought. She was feeling unattractive because of the advanced stage of her pregnancy. She had gained only a few pounds over what Dr. Meyers recommended, but on her petite frame it did seem more. Her slender face had filled out. She even had a bit of a double chin. And since her bones were so small and delicate, her legs and arms remained slender while her belly dominated her whole body.

He grasped her by the shoulders and refused to release her when she tried to pull away. He forcefully turned her around to face him, but she bent her head and looked straight down.

"You don't know, do you?" He lifted her off the bed and onto his lap, then placed his arm around her waist. "You really have no idea how beautiful you are to me." He loosened the tie belt and spread apart her pink satin robe, revealing her enlarged breasts and big tummy.

She gasped and tried to pull her robe closed, but Adam would have none of it. "Don't try to hide your body from me when I love to look at it."

"How can you possibly love looking at me when I'm so big and fat and—"

"Don't you dare say that you're ugly." Adam slipped the robe off her shoulders, letting it puddle around her hips. "You're beautiful. Your body has changed to accommodate that big boy growing inside you." He caressed her stomach. Her breathing accelerated. "But those changes don't make you ugly. How could any man look at a woman whose body was ripening with his child and not see the most beautiful sight in the world?"

She draped her arms around Adam's neck, buried her face in his shoulder and cried softly while he rubbed her back. "You're such an old-fashioned man," she said. "You know that don't you? You're like some damned knight in shining armor, always trying to protect and defend and rescue me . . . whether or not I want to be rescued."

"I'm trying to do better." He nuzzled her neck, then kissed her ear. "Honest, babe. I am trying."

"Don't you dare apologize for being so wonderful to me!" She wrapped herself around him, her fat belly pressed against his flat stomach, and kissed him, devoured him, consumed all the heat and passion he felt.

Easing her down on the bed, Adam hovered over her, staring at her with desire burning in his eyes. "You are the most exciting, desirable woman I've ever known." His hands moved over her body with an almost reverent homage. "Let me love you, Blythe. Let me show you just how beautiful you are to me."

She gave herself over to his masterful touch, glorying in the wild and marvelously wonderful sensations spiraling through her. His mouth found and savored each special, sensitive spot on her body. His lips feasted on her breasts. His tongue painted a hot, moist trail downward, zeroing in on its target found hidden between the folds of her femininity. When he touched her there, she moaned, lifting her hips up off the bed.

Making love to a woman had never been this important to Adam. He needed to give Blythe the sweetest loving she'd ever known and prove to her that she was irresistible to him. And heaven help him, that's exactly what she was. He hadn't been able to resist her—those big hazel eyes, that full, pouty mouth, that hot woman's body, delicate and yet strong.

The heart of her body was sweet, intoxicating and smelled of jasmine and musk. He loved the taste of her, loved listening to her panting moans, and loved the feel of her body quivering under his tongue.

Blythe could not stop the tidal wave of completion as it swept over her, thrashing her about like flotsam after a storm. When the aftershocks of release rippled through her, Adam turned her onto her side and fitted his body, spoon-fashion, against hers. Lifting her slightly, he entered her and within moments lost himself completely in his own strong release.

Adam lifted the tray containing the remnants of their meal off the floor and set it on the hearth. Bracing his back against the right bottom side of the sofa, he reached out, put his arms around Blythe and dragged her backward, fitting her hips between his spread legs.

She leaned her head back to rest on his chest, and gazed into the crackling fire Adam had built in the fireplace before they ate dinner. She loved evenings at home alone with her husband. Her temporary husband, she reminded herself and sighed, wishing their marriage was real, wishing Adam would be her husband for the next hundred years or so.

"So, what do you think of the house plans?" he asked.

Adam pulled the blueprints off the coffee table where he'd laid them earlier when he'd first shown them to her. Placing them in her lap, he held each end so that the paper wouldn't curl back into a roll.

"I think this place is way too big for just me and Elliott. There's over five thousand square feet. It's a mansion, not a house."

"You don't like it?"

"Of course I like it." She cuddled against him, nuzzling her head against his naked chest. "It's fantastic. My dream house. All those windows. All that open space, upstairs and down. But it will cost a fortune to build."

"You let me worry about the cost. Nothing is too good for you . . . and Elliott."

"When you promised to build me a house, I never expected something like this."

"So, you like it?"

"Yes, I love it."

"Look it over and decide if you want any changes," he said. "I want this house to be perfect. You deserve nothing less."

"When Elliott gets older and spends more time with you, I'll get lonesome in such a big place." She laid her hands atop his where they held open the house plans. "I'll just rattle around in it, listening to the echo of my own voice."

"That'll be years from now." Adam leaned his head over and caressed the side of her face with his cheek. "While Elliott's little, he'll be with you most of the time. I'd like it if you'd let me stop by and see him every day, maybe have dinner with you sometimes."

"You can stop by anytime you want." Tonight had been almost perfect. She didn't want to discuss the future and ruin their ephemeral happiness. But the end of their marriage wasn't that far off. The only sensible thing to do was make plans for it. "Any time you want to come by, you'll be welcome. You never have to call or anything."

"You might change your mind when you—" he swallowed down his anger and frustration at the thought "—start dating again."

Dating again! Never! Not in a million years. How could she ever want another man after being Adam's wife? "Well, that'll be a long time in the future, too. I'll be too busy with Elliott to think much about dating. Of course, you'll be the most eligible bachelor in the state again once the divorce goes through."

There had been a time when he'd enjoyed his bachelor status, with a delightful selection of ladies from which to choose. But his feelings about bachelorhood had changed since his marriage to Blythe. Despite her lack of domesticity, she'd made coming home something to look forward to. Hell, it had even gotten to the point where he enjoyed their arguments. Mainly because they usually made up in bed.

"I'm not going to rush back into dating, either," he admitted. "I'd like to spend all my free time with my son, especially when he's a baby. I don't want to miss anything." Adam took the house plans, rolled them up and tossed them onto the coffee table. "Blythe, what if, after the divorce, I might want to stay the night with Elliott sometime? Would you mind?"

"No..." She cleared her throat. "No, of course I wouldn't mind."

"And any time you need a baby-sitter, I'd come over," he said. "You know, if you needed to work late or—"

She turned in his arms, placed her finger over his lips and smiled. "We're going to raise Elliott together. The one thing we've always agreed on, since the day we married, is that our child isn't going to suffer because his parents are divorced."

"You know I had my doubts when we got married. I wondered if we'd be able to work things out." Adam kissed her on the nose. "But now I know one thing. We're going to come out of this marriage as good friends, and we're going to be good parents, whether we stay married or not."

"Whether we stay married?"

"Forget I said that. It was a slip of the tongue. I know neither of us wants to stay married for our child's sake."

"Oh. Yes, of course, you're right." What had she hoped he'd meant? Had she really hoped that he might be having second thoughts about their relationship? Yes, dammit! Yes! She *had* hoped that maybe, just maybe, Adam Wyatt was falling in love with her. But that wasn't going to happen. She had his respect, his devotion and his friendship— and the pleasure of his body on a temporary basis. Anything else would be asking for too much.

# Eleven

"**A**dam Wyatt taking Lamaze classes. I'd like to see that!" Joy Simpson positioned a yellow carnation in the floral arrangement on which she was working. "The Playboy of the South helping his wife learn how to huff and puff during delivery. Oh, how the mighty have fallen."

"Will you stop teasing Blythe." Martha Jean laid a dozen red roses on the work counter and began separating them. "I've always heard that reformed playboys make the most devoted husbands. Kind of like the way reformed sinners become religious fanatics."

"He's really trying to tone down his enthusiasm for fatherhood," Blythe said. "But it's difficult for Adam to control his excitement. You'd think I was the only woman in the world who's ever had a baby."

"You're the only woman in the world who's ever had his baby," Joy reminded her.

Shivers of awareness rippled up Blythe's spine. She had become more aware with each passing day just how much

Adam wanted their child, that he truly looked forward to being a father. Was that the reason he was so good to her, the reason he seemed to dote on her, fulfilling her every wish, complying to her every whim? Of course it was. What other reason could there be? He knew that a happy, healthy, content mother was important to his child's well-being, before and after birth.

"I think it's adorable the way Mr. Wyatt spoils Blythe," Martha Jean said. "It's plain to see he's madly in love with her. He just lights up like a Christmas tree every time he looks at her."

Blythe noticed the pity in Joy's eyes as their gazes met. Only Joy and Craig knew that her marriage was not a love match, that in a few short months her *doting* husband was going to divorce her.

"I'm starving to death," Blythe said. "I stay hungry all the time. I'm going to take a break."

She rushed into the back storeroom, holding the tears inside until she'd closed herself in the bathroom. She slumped over the sink, turned on the faucets and dampened a washcloth. Glancing in the mirror she gasped when she saw her pale, sad face.

How could she be so miserable when to the outside world her life seemed perfect? She was married to a man everyone thought worshiped the ground she walked on. She was nearly seven and a half months pregnant with a child both she and her husband wanted. And in a few short months, she would be moving into her dream house, a mansion her husband was sparing no expense to build for her.

How could she possibly be unhappy when she had everything? Everything except the one thing she wanted most—Adam's love.

If eight months ago someone had told her that she would share a night of wild passion with Adam Wyatt, conceive his child, marry him and then fall head over heels in love with him, she would have told them they were crazy. Her life had changed drastically in such a short period of time, and even bigger changes were in store for her.

There were times when she came close to telling Adam that she didn't want a divorce, that she wanted them to stay married and raise Elliott together. But then she realized he might agree to her request, and she'd end up spending the rest of her life married to a man who didn't love her.

Blythe's stomach growled. Darn! She'd eaten a huge breakfast around seven this morning and here it was—she checked her wristwatch—barely ten-thirty and she felt as if she hadn't eaten in days. She had gained five pounds more than she should have, and Dr. Meyers had scolded her. Then Adam started watching every bite that went into her mouth. And they had wound up having more than one heated argument over the fact that she thought Dr. Meyers and Adam were treating her like a child. Those arguments had ended, as all their arguments did, in bed.

Blythe smiled. Adam was a genius at figuring out ways to have sex while protecting her protruding stomach. Their lovemaking was slower, sweeter, more gentle and yet complete and satisfying. She blushed when she remembered the things Adam said and did to her—and she to him.

Blythe felt a sudden gush of liquid between her legs. Gasping, she pressed her legs together tightly and clutched her stomach. Dear God, surely her water hadn't broken. Not yet. She was only seven months into her pregnancy.

She made her way over to the commode, sat down and lifted her maternity jumper. Bright red blood stained the inside of her thighs. Trembling, Blythe opened her mouth in a silent scream, the sound lodging in her throat. What was wrong? She shouldn't be bleeding! Was she losing the baby? How could she be bleeding when there was no pain?

"Joy!" Blythe screamed. "Joy, come here!"

The bathroom door flew open and Joy rushed in, Martha Jean right behind her.

"What's wrong?" Joy asked.

"I'm bleeding," Blythe said. "I'm bleeding a lot."

"Don't panic." Joy gripped Blythe's shoulder. "Stay calm." Joy turned to Martha Jean. "Call Dr. Meyers and tell him that Blythe Wyatt is bleeding badly and I'm taking her straight to Decatur General. Then call Adam and tell him to meet us there. But try not to frighten him."

"Do you need any help getting Blythe to your car?" Ringing her hands, Martha Jean hovered in the doorway.

"No, I can handle things. Just go make those phone calls." Joy slipped her arm around Blythe's waist and helped her stand. "Can you walk?"

"Yes, I—I'm not hurting. I'm just bleeding. And it won't stop." Blythe clutched Joy's forearms and gazed into her friend's stricken face. "I can't lose this baby. I can't! You just don't know what Elliott means to us. To me. And to Adam. He'll die if anything happens to his son."

With her arm around Blythe's thick waist, Joy jerked a hand towel off the rack and handed it to Blythe, then led her out of the bathroom. Martha Jean, talking on the cordless phone to Dr. Meyers's office, opened the front door and walked out into the cold February morning with Blythe and Joy. She followed them over to Joy's black Chrysler.

"Yes, yes. I'll tell her." Martha Jean leaned into the front seat and clasped Blythe's trembling hands. "Dr. Meyers will meet y'all at the hospital."

"Call Adam," Blythe said. "Please, I want Adam."

"I'll call him right now." Martha Jean closed the passenger side door and stepped back, then punched the numbers for Wyatt Construction and lifted the phone to her ear.

She waved goodbye as Joy backed her New Yorker out of the parking lot and headed up Second Avenue. Sandra Pennington answered Adam's private line.

"Please tell Mr. Wyatt to hurry to Decatur General," Martha Jean said. "There's an emergency with his wife."

Adam stormed into the hospital like a marauding barbarian, barking questions, shouting demands and stomping past all the hospital personnel trying to stop him. He saw

Joy Simpson standing in the hallway, her makeup streaked with dried tears.

"Is Blythe all right?" Adam growled the question.

Joy nodded her head. "For now."

"Where is she?"

When he looked toward the nearest closed door, Joy grabbed his arm. "Dr. Meyers is in there with her now."

"I want to see her."

"Adam, you've got to calm down," Joy said. "It won't help Blythe, or the baby, for her to see you this upset."

"What the hell happened? She's been fine. Better than fine. Not one problem." Adam spread his palms flat against the door frame, then pressed his forehead against the door. His big body shook. He gripped the door frame to steady his shaky hands.

Joy placed her hand on Adam's back, patting him gently. "I don't know what happened. She just started bleeding."

Adam spun around, grabbed Joy by the shoulders and glared into her eyes. "She was bleeding? How bad was it?"

"Adam..."

"How bad?"

"Pretty bad," Joy admitted, then pulled away from Adam and turned her head.

Adam gripped her shoulder. "I can't stand out here waiting, not knowing. If they want to keep me away from her, they're going to have to knock me unconscious."

He squeezed Joy's quivering shoulder, released her and grabbed the door handle. He eased the door open despite his desire to kick the damn thing from its hinges.

Dr. Meyers, who stood at the foot of the bed and blocked Blythe from Adam's view, turned sharply when the door opened, then smiled weakly and waved for Adam to enter.

"Come on in," Dr. Meyers said. "You're the one person she wants to see."

Adam rushed to Blythe's bedside. The attending nurse jumped aside to prevent his knocking her down.

"Babe? I'm here." Adam reached down and lifted her hand in his.

Despite her round face and fat tummy, Blythe looked so small and delicate lying there in the hospital bed, her red hair strikingly bright against the pristine white pillowcase. Her face was so pale. Her makeup was a tearstained mess.

She squeezed his hand. "I was so scared. I don't want to lose Elliott. I can't . . . can't . . ."

"Hush, babe. Hush. Don't even think it." Adam looked at Dr. Meyers. "Nothing's going to happen to you or Elliott."

"I shouldn't have started calling him by his name, should I?" Clinging to Adam's hand, she lifted it to her abdomen. "Giving him a name made him a real person, and now if . . . if . . ." She burst into tears.

Adam sat down on the edge of the bed and took his wife in his arms. He gazed up at the doctor, unconcerned that the man would see tears in his eyes.

"Blythe. Adam," Dr. Meyers said.

With Adam's reassuring arms around her, Blythe swallowed her tears. Adam wiped her face with his fingertips.

"Blythe has developed what is known as placenta previa."

Blythe and Adam stared at the doctor, their heartbeats accelerating as fear spiraled through them.

"I know it sounds like some sort of disease," Dr. Meyers said. "But it isn't. At this late stage of your pregnancy, the placenta should have moved upward and away from the mouth of the uterus, but instead it is still covering the edge of the os—the mouth of the uterus. In fact, the placenta is actually touching the os, and that's what's causing the bleeding."

"How serious is this condition?" Blythe asked. "Is El . . . our baby in danger?"

"Your pregnancy is in its thirty-second week, so if we have to take the baby, he should survive," Dr. Meyers explained. "But we're going to do everything possible to avoid doing a C-section now, so we can let your baby do a bit more growing.''

"What can you do?'' Blythe hugged Adam, sighing as she absorbed the comfort of being in his strong arms.

"We're going to keep you in the hospital for a few days. You're to stay in bed, except for bathroom privileges. We'll carefully monitor the situation, give you extra iron and vitamin C and, if necessary…'' Dr. Meyers hesitated. "If the bleeding continues, we'll have to give you blood transfusions.''

Blythe nodded her head. "I'll do whatever is necessary for the baby.''

"Is there any danger for Blythe?'' Adam asked, stroking his wife's back, wishing more than anything he could do something—anything—to keep her safe and well.

"Ninety-nine percent of women today who have placenta previa come through okay, as well as their babies.'' Dr. Meyers walked over and patted Adam on the back. "We're going to take good care of Blythe, and if she improves, she might be able to go home in a week or so. Of course, she'll have to stay in bed, and someone will have to be with her twenty-four hours a day.''

"If she's allowed to go home, I'll be there with her all the time,'' Adam said.

"But you can't do that,'' Blythe told him. "You can't possibly stay away from Wyatt Construction for weeks. We can hire someone. A nurse.''

"I can run the business from the house, if necessary.'' Easing Blythe down onto the bed, he held her gently by the shoulders. "I'll hire around-the-clock nurses for you when you come home. But if you think I'm going to leave you alone for one minute, you'd better think again. Nothing is more important to me than you and Elliott.''

Tears choked Blythe. Closing her eyes, she turned her face into her pillow and cried.

Adam walked Dr. Meyers out of the room and asked him if he'd been totally honest with them about Blythe's condition. Joy walked over to where the two men stood talking.

"I was completely honest with you," Dr. Meyers said. "We want to do everything possible to bring this pregnancy to term, but if the hemorrhaging worsens, we'll have no choice but to do a C-section."

"May I go in to see Blythe?" Joy asked.

"Go right on in," the doctor told her, then turned to Adam. "If you'd like to stay the night with Blythe, I can arrange it."

"Arrange for me to stay as long as she's in here," Adam said.

Dr. Meyers shook his head and laughed. "I'd tell you that you can't do that, but knowing you and the way you feel about your wife, I realize it would be useless. Just try not to antagonize the entire hospital staff while you're playing nursemaid."

Adam was well aware of the fact that the staff of Decatur General prayed to see the end of him. In the two weeks since Blythe's admission, he hadn't left the hospital. He ate his meals with her, showered and shaved in her bathroom, had a separate business phone line put in and oversaw everything that concerned Blythe's care. No one could budge Adam. None of Joy's and Craig's attempts to persuade him to leave had worked. And Dr. Meyers's subtle threats hadn't been effective. Even when Blythe begged him to go home, he had refused.

And now he was glad he hadn't been swayed by other people's tactics. What if he'd been miles away at a construction sight when Blythe had begun to hemorrhage so heavily that Dr. Meyers decided he had no choice but to do immediate surgery?

She was in her thirty-fourth week of pregnancy. Dr. Meyers had said he didn't foresee any complications, but he had alerted the NICU at Huntsville Hospital, just in case.

Joy and Craig found Adam sitting alone in the waiting room, his hands between his spread knees, his head bowed. Joy sat down on one side of him, Craig on the other.

"Any word yet?" Craig asked.

"Not yet." Adam didn't look up, he just kept staring down at the floor.

"Everything is going to be all right," Joy assured him. "Dr. Meyers is one of the best obstetricians in the state. He'll bring Blythe and the baby through just fine."

"He'd better." Adam growled the words deep and low. "If anything happens to her..."

Joy patted Adam on the back. "I'll go get us some coffee." She signaled to Craig that he should reassure Adam, then she stood. "I'll be right back."

When Joy disappeared around the corner, Craig cleared his throat. Adam didn't respond. Craig grunted.

"It's all right," Adam said. "You don't have to try to cheer me up. I know Joy thinks there's something you can say to me that will help me stop worrying. Well, there isn't."

"Yeah, I know there isn't." Craig stuck his hands in his pockets and leaned back on the sofa. "If it was Joy in there, I'd be half out of my mind, just the way you are."

"I don't know how it happened. I don't even know when it happened. But somewhere between the night I got Blythe pregnant and tonight when they wheeled her into surgery, I fell in love with that woman."

Craig chuckled. "Are you just now realizing that fact? Hell, man, everybody else has known it for months."

"What do you mean everybody else has known?"

"Me. Joy. Martha Jean. Sandra. Dr. Meyers. Every employee of Decatur General."

"Has it been that obvious?"

"Yeah, to everyone but your wife. You haven't told her, have you?"

"No, dammit. She went into surgery not knowing how I really feel." Adam shot up off the sofa and paced back and forth in the small waiting area. "Hell, I didn't even admit it to myself until... I'm not giving her a divorce. I don't care if she throws a fit. I don't care what she threatens to do. I'm never going to let her walk out of my life and into another man's arms.''

"Mr. Wyatt?" A tall, slender nurse called his name.

Adam rushed over to her. Craig stood and walked across the room.

"Yes, I'm Adam Wyatt."

"Dr. Meyers would like to see you. If you'll come with me."

"Is something wrong?" Adam asked. "Is Blythe all right?"

Adam had never been so afraid in his entire life. If anything had happened to Blythe, he didn't think he could bear to go on living.

# Twelve

———

"**Y**our wife is fine, Mr. Wyatt." The nurse smiled.

Letting out the breath he'd been holding, Adam suddenly felt light-headed.

"Dr. Meyers thought you might want to come into surgery and be present at your son's birth."

"What? Is that possible? My wife is having a cesarean."

"Yes, I know. But Dr. Meyers is the kind of obstetrician who doesn't mind making the birth process a family affair."

"You mean I can actually go in there and be with Blythe during the surgery."

"If you'd like," the nurse said. "But you'll have to hurry. Your wife has already been prepped and given an epidural."

Craig walked over and put his arm around Adam's shoulder. "It's the experience of a lifetime. I'll never forget the day Missy was born. It's a special memory Joy and I will share forever."

"God, Craig, I'm scared."

Craig laughed. "So was I. But Blythe will be strong enough for both of you." Craig turned to the nurse. "Did Mrs. Wyatt tell Dr. Meyers she wanted her husband with her?"

"She insisted," the nurse said. "Please, Mr. Wyatt, let's go. We'll have to get you suited up."

Adam followed the nurse's instructions, suited up in sterile garb and went into surgery. Blythe lay on the operating table, drapes arranged around her exposed abdomen and an IV connected to her left hand.

"I'm here, babe," he told her as he sat in a chair that had been placed near her head.

She held up her right hand. Clasping it gently, he brought it to his mouth for a kiss.

"I told Dr. Meyers I wasn't going to have this baby without you," Blythe said. "Our bargain was that we'd share everything."

"Thank you." He whispered the words against her ear.

The surgery took about ten minutes. Just before Elliott Adam Wyatt was eased from his mother's body, Blythe asked that the screen protecting Adam and her from viewing the graphic details of the surgery be lowered enough to allow them to see the actual birth.

Adam watched while the nurse suctioned his son's nose and mouth. Elliott let out a loud cry. Adam's heart stopped for one brief moment. Tears momentarily clouded his vision. Blythe squeezed his hand.

While the nurse put Elliott through the normal routine for newborns, Dr. Meyers attended to Blythe. She and Adam couldn't take their eyes off their son, the most wonderful, precious thing either of them had ever seen.

"May I hold him?" Blythe asked Dr. Meyers, who immediately motioned for the nurse.

"Give Elliott to his father," Dr. Meyers said. "Y'all can hold him briefly, then we want to get him into the ICU nursery."

"ICU nursery?" Blythe squeezed her husband's hand. "What's wrong? Is Elliott—"

"Elliott appears to be just fine, especially for a premature infant," the doctor said. "Sending him to the ICU nursery is strictly standard procedure."

The nurse handed Elliott, wrapped in a soft blue blanket, to his father. Adam stared down at the infant in his arms. His son. The tears brimming in Adam's eyes spilled over and streamed down his cheeks. Sitting beside Blythe, he placed their baby into his mother's waiting arms.

Blythe held Elliott, noting every feature of his tiny face. She slipped her index finger into his hand, smiling when he instinctively twined his little fingers around hers.

"He's beautiful. Isn't he?" She glanced up at Adam and saw that he was crying. Adam Wyatt. Her big, macho husband was weeping with the joy of fatherhood.

Grinning, Adam licked the tears off his mouth. He reached over and caressed the sparse strands of hair on Elliott's tiny round head. "He's got your hair. Kind of a coppery red."

The nurse leaned over and took Elliott. "Y'all will get to see plenty of him. We'll bring him to your room later, Mrs. Wyatt."

"You get some rest, Blythe," Dr. Meyers told her, then turned to Adam. "You go get some coffee, hand out cigars and make a few phone calls. By then Blythe will be in her room, and if everything checks out with Elliott, y'all can see him again."

Once back in her room, Adam stayed with Blythe, holding her hand, resting his head on her pillow when she dozed off to sleep. He didn't know how Blythe would react when he told her that he'd changed his mind about the divorce, that he could not—would not—let her go. He had to find a way to approach the subject without antagonizing her, without making her feel as if he weren't giving her a choice in the matter. And that was the problem. He didn't intend to give her a choice in the matter. There was no way he was going to lose this woman!

Blythe's hospital room looked as if half her florist shop had been transported there. Adam, typically old-fashioned, overpowering man that he was, had surrounded her with every luxury. In the three days since Elliott's birth, Adam had been at her side constantly, except for a trip home every afternoon to shower, shave, change clothes and make a few business calls. He seemed unable to drag himself away from her and Elliott. She had known he would be possessive of Elliott, but she had never dreamed he would shower her with so much attention after their child was born.

Dr. Meyers had been pleased with her recovery and surprised at Elliott's nearly six-pound birth weight. He had told Blythe that her son might have weighed nine pounds if he hadn't been a few weeks premature. Since she and Elliott were doing so well, they were going home this afternoon.

Home with Adam. For a few more weeks.

Blythe tried not to think about how soon she and Adam would end their marriage and she and Elliott would move into the beautiful mansion Adam had built for them. If only she could be with Adam, she'd gladly live in a two-room shack.

The nurse helped Blythe dress Elliott in the blue-and-white going-home outfit she and Adam had chosen on one of their many shopping sprees. Adam waited impatiently in the doorway, shifting his weight from one foot to the other.

Something was wrong. Blythe had sensed it the moment he'd arrived today. Adam was nervous. And Adam was never nervous. He was often agitated, occasionally aggravated or angry, but he wasn't the nervous type.

She knew nothing was wrong with Elliott. Dr. Wilson, the pediatrician she and Adam had chosen, had given their son a clean bill of health. Dr. Meyers had said she'd come through the cesarean without any complications and if she took good care of herself and followed his instructions, she would recover completely in no time. So, if Elliott was fine and she was fine, then the problem had to be with Adam.

Maybe he was eager to set the wheels in motion to end their marriage. Maybe he wanted to discuss their divorce, but didn't want to upset her so soon after surgery and Elliott's birth.

On the ride home, Adam was unusually quiet. Blythe tried to engage him in conversation about Elliott, about his business, about Elliott, about her business, even about the weather—everything and anything except their marriage.

The nurse Adam had hired met them in the driveway, took Elliott from the car seat in the back and carried him inside. Blythe would be glad when she had recovered enough from the surgery to lift Elliott without any help. Adam came around to the passenger side of the car—a new Mercedes he'd bought to accommodate an infant car seat—opened the door and scooped Blythe up in his arms.

"Are you warm enough?" He glanced at her simple wool coat. She had refused to let him buy her a fur of any kind. "Do you need a blanket?"

"I'll be fine from here to the house," she assured him.

He carried her inside, straight to her bedroom, which was filled with pink roses. Her favorite flower. He deposited her on the side of the bed, then helped her out of her coat.

She glanced around the room, taking special note of the bassinet she had asked Adam to place by the side of the bed. Even if he had insisted on a nurse to help her with Elliott, she intended to have her son at her side during the night. Adam had made no protest and had agreed he'd lift Elliott into her arms until she could do it herself.

"I want Elliott in here now," she said.

"Ms. Hobart will bring him to you in a little while," Adam told her. "I need to talk to you first."

Blythe's heart caught in her throat. Here it comes, she thought. He's going to ask me to sign the divorce papers today so that by the time of my six-week checkup, he can leave me and resume the life he led before I trapped him into marriage.

How could he be so heartless? So callous? To ask her for a divorce, today of all days? How would she get through this without bursting into tears? She had no idea how she'd survive without breaking down, but she couldn't do that. If she did, he'd know she loved him and wanted to be his wife forever.

"What do you want to talk to me about?" she asked, but couldn't bring herself to look at him.

Adam bent down on one knee, removed Blythe's slippers, then stood, pulled the covers down and lifted her into the middle of the bed. He fluffed the pillows at her back.

"Are you comfortable?" he asked.

"I'm fine. What do you want to talk to me about?"

Adam walked over to the vanity stool where he had laid his briefcase, picked it up, opened it and removed the legal document from inside. "I want to discuss our divorce."

She went cold all over, despite the cosy warmth of her bedroom. A tight fist clutched her heart. She shouldn't be surprised. It was what she'd expected.

"Our divorce?" she said. "We agreed to divorce after the baby was born and he and I had our six-week checkups."

"That's what we agreed to before we married." Holding the document in his hand, Adam sat down on the bed beside Blythe.

"Yes, we agreed to the divorce, and we agreed to share custody of Elliott. But you said I could keep him with me for the first year. Have you changed your mind?"

"I've changed my mind about a lot of things," he told her.

Tears of disappointment and anger filled her eyes. Had all of Adam's kindness, all his loving concern, all his possessive protectiveness been a lie? Did he want a divorce immediately? Did he want to begin the joint custody right now? Was that why he'd insisted on hiring a nurse?

"I should have known," she said softly, and swallowed her tears.

He turned and saw her pale face, her trembling chin, the teardrops clinging to her lashes. "Blythe... babe... what's wrong? What did I say to upset you?" He gently grasped her shoulders.

She glared at him as tears trickled down her cheeks. "Don't be nice to me. Don't you dare be nice to me! You want a divorce? Well, give me the damn papers to sign. I'll give you your divorce. But you are not going to take Elliott. Not now. Not even if you have a dozen nurses to take care of him. You promised me that I could keep him the first year. We had a bargain."

Adam grinned, his heart swelling with hope. Dear God, he had tried to figure out a way to approach this subject, to tell her that he planned to break their agreement. He'd been so afraid she wouldn't want to stay married to him, and now here she was practically throwing a fit because she thought he wanted a divorce immediately.

He tightened his hold on her shoulders. "I'm never going to take Elliott away from you. That's a promise."

She gazed directly into his black eyes and wasn't sure if she could believe what she saw. "Are you saying that you don't want joint custody anymore?"

"I'm saying that..." If she took offense at what he was about to say, he'd have to deal with it later. He was who he was, and he couldn't go about this differently. He damn well didn't want to give her a choice in the matter. "There isn't going to be a divorce. I'm not letting you go. Even if you think we can't make our marriage work, I'm going to prove to you that we can. Elliott doesn't need to live with his father part of the time and his mother part of the time. He needs to grow up in a home where his parents are together."

Blythe stared at Adam for several seconds, then blinked away her tears. "You want us to stay married for Elliott?" This was what she'd been afraid might happen if she ever gave Adam any encouragement. But she didn't want to remain married to a man for the sake of their child. She wanted, she needed—no, she *had to have* his love.

"Elliott doesn't need parents trying to live together, trying to make a marriage work, when they don't love each other." She cupped Adam's cheek with her hand. "No matter how hard we tried, it just wouldn't work."

"Even if you don't love me now, you might learn to love me. Eventually." Releasing her shoulder, he covered her hand with his. "I know I'm not your ideal man, but I'll try my best not to drive you crazy with my unacceptable behavior. And we have a lot more in common than either of us realized. Not to mention Elliott."

He eased his hand around to grasp the back of her neck. Drawing her mouth up to his, he sighed against her lips. "And the sex between us is incredible," he said. "That's more than a lot of couples have."

She was tempted, so very, very tempted. "Oh, Adam." She kissed him. Light. Sweet. Quick. "How could we spend the rest of our lives together without love?"

"You don't think there's any way you could ever love me?" he asked.

She saw the look in his eyes again, that unbelievable look that made her stomach flutter and her heart fill with hope. "Me, love you? Oh, Adam."

He released her and turned his back, slumping his shoulders. "Yeah, I guess it's too much to hope that you could ever love me the way I love you."

"What?" Despite the achy pull of her stitches, she scooted over to him, wrapped her arms around his waist, and laid her head on his back. "Would you repeat that, please?"

He tensed, his body going completely rigid. "Yeah, it was pretty stupid of me, wasn't it, to go and fall in love with you, when I knew how you felt about—"

"But I do love you, Adam," she said, her face pressed against his back. "I started falling in love with you not long after we got married."

He whipped around, took her in his arms and stared into her moist hazel eyes. "You love me?"

"Yes, I love you, you big dope." She smiled through her tears. "I can't believe you hadn't already figured it out. I mean, every time you touch me, I fall to pieces."

"I thought it was just sex," he said. "On both our parts. Wild, wonderful and fabulous, but just sex. At least, I kept telling myself that's all it was."

"When did you realize it was more than sex...that it was love?"

"God, woman, if you hadn't just had a baby, just had surgery, I'd make love to you all day and night." He slipped his arms beneath her, lifted her gently and set her down in the middle of the bed, placing her back against the pillows. He cupped her face with his hands. "I told Craig, right before Elliott was born, that I loved you, but I'd figured it out weeks ago. The day Joy had to rush you to the hospital. For a little while there, I was afraid I might lose you. The truth hit me like a ton of bricks. My life wouldn't be worth a damn without you, babe."

She draped her arms around his neck. "Do you think maybe we've been in love all along? I mean, even before we got married? Maybe even that first night we spent together, when I conceived Elliott?"

"Yeah, I figure it was love at first sight for both of us, and we let all our prejudices get in the way." He leaned her into the pillows, kissing her slowly, lingering over each touch. "I'll be crazy by the time the doctor gives us the okay to make love again."

"Well, you're very resourceful when it comes to figuring out how to get things accomplished." She tiptoed her fingers down his chest, across his taut abdomen and across the crotch of his slacks.

His arousal strained upward against her hand. "Don't tempt me, babe. Not until you can make good on that silent promise you just made, and not until I can love you the way you deserve to be loved."

"That could be weeks and weeks." She cuddled against him, sighing with happiness when he wrapped her tenderly in his arms.

"I won't like having to wait, but I'll manage somehow. If I can hold you in my arms and kiss you, and sleep by your side every night, and help you take care of our son, it will be enough for the time being."

"You're lying." She laughed, the sound free and joyous. "But I love you for it."

"And I love you, babe. I love you more than anything in this world."

An hour later Nurse Hobart woke Mr. and Mrs. Wyatt, who had fallen asleep in each other's arms.

"I'm so sorry to bother you," she said. "But Elliott is hungry, and he's making quite a fuss about it."

Blythe unzipped her purple velvet caftan, released the catch on the cup of her nursing bra and held out her arms for Elliott. Nurse Hobart handed him to his mother, then left the room and closed the door behind her.

Adam sat up straight in the bed, placed his arms around Blythe and watched his son suck greedily at her breast. A feeling like none other he'd ever experienced settled over him. A sense of happiness so sweet he wanted to capture the moment and save it forever.

"We have it all, Adam," Blythe said. "Everything that really matters."

"Amen to that, babe."

# Epilogue

"The only thing I can compare a birthday party at the Wyatts' to is a three-ring circus," Joy Simpson said as she handed out Popsicles to the children running up and down the huge patio at the back of the elegant brick home Adam had built Blythe over eight years ago.

"Well, if they'd been sensible and stopped having children after the first two, the way we did, they wouldn't have this problem," Craig said.

"The children aren't a problem." Blythe smiled at Craig, then readjusted her year-old daughter on her hip. "Our problem is Adam finding time to run Wyatt Construction while I operate two businesses and we make time to be good parents. Thank goodness Martha Jean can run Petals Plus on her own most of the time. And the kids love spending time with me at my Flower Garden Nursery."

"I believe Joy and Craig think we have too many kids, babe. What do you think?" Adam held out his arms for his youngest child. "Come to Daddy, birthday girl."

"Well, if Adam hadn't had his heart set on having a daughter, we might have stopped after the boys." Blythe handed Rachel Alana Wyatt to her father. "Toby and Max are a handful, like most twins, but when they were four, we decided to give it one more try."

"Thank goodness you had Rachel." Joy laughed. "Or y'all might have wound up with your own baseball team."

Adam rubbed noses with his little girl. Rachel giggled, shaking her head, her black curls bouncing. She smiled at her daddy, two sets of sable brown eyes meeting.

"Yeah, if you'd had a girl first the way we did, you could have avoided having to send four kids through college." Laughing, Craig Simpson slapped his best friend on the back. "Lucky for you you're a damned millionaire."

"Lucky for me I've got Blythe for their mother." Adam draped his arm around his wife's shoulders, pulling her against him as they watched their three rowdy sons running around in the backyard, chasing nine-year-old Missy Simpson, while her younger brother joined in the fun.

"Yeah, we're both a couple of lucky guys," Craig said. "Despite what we got stuck with. Beautiful, loving wives and healthy, happy children."

"Oh, yeah. Just look what Joy and I got stuck with." Blythe gazed up at her husband, her eyes filled with adoration. "A couple of old-fashioned, macho studs!"

All four adults laughed, each one silently thanking the Lord above for their many blessings.

\* \* \* \* \*

**♥ SILHOUETTE**

*Desire*

## COMING NEXT MONTH

### TALLCHIEF'S BRIDE  Cait London

*Man of the Month*

The legend said that when a Tallchief placed the ring on the right woman's finger, he would capture true love. Talia Petrovna had gone to the ends of the earth to find Calum Tallchief's ring—but was a woman like her truly fated to be his bride?

### A BRIDE FOR ABEL GREENE  Cindy Gerard

*Northern Lights Brides*

Mail-order bride Mackenzie Kincaid had prepared herself for a loveless marriage to Abel Greene. Now Abel was hesitant; he wanted out of the deal. If Mackenzie wanted to stay wedded, she *had* to seduce her husband!

### LOVERS ONLY  Christine Pacheco

Workaholic Clay Landon was so caught up in securing the future that he'd neglected the present—and his wife, Catherine. Could Clay win her back and fulfil her dreams of raising his children?

### ROXY AND THE RICH MAN  Elizabeth Bevarly

*The Family McCormick*

Wealthy businessman Spencer Melbourne hired private investigator Roxy Matheny to find his long-lost twin. Roxy knew she was in over her head— she could give him what he needed professionally, but what about more *personalized* services?

### CITY GIRLS NEED NOT APPLY  Rita Rainville

Rugged single-father Mac Ryder knew that city girl Kathryn Wainwright wasn't prepared for the dangers of Wyoming. However, Kathryn knew that the confirmed bachelor was really the one in danger—of settling down with her!

### REBEL'S SPIRIT  Susan Connell

Raleigh Hanlon hadn't seen the mischievous Rebecca Barnett in ten years, but now she was home again. Her zest for life had captivated him and he'd stopped even trying to keep her—and his imagination—under control!

# COMING NEXT MONTH FROM

 SILHOUETTE®

## Sensation

*A thrilling mix of passion, adventure and drama*

**AT THE MIDNIGHT HOUR** Alicia Scott
**MUMMY'S HERO** Audra Adams
**MAN WITHOUT A MEMORY** Maura Seger
**MEGAN'S MATE** Nora Roberts

## Intrigue

*Danger, deception and desire*

**GUARDED MOMENTS** Cassie Miles
**BULLETPROOF HEART** Sheryl Lynn
**EDGE OF ETERNITY** Jasmine Cresswell
**NO WAY OUT** Tina Vasilos

## Special Edition

*Satisfying romances packed with emotion*

**MUM FOR HIRE** Victoria Pade
**THE FATHER NEXT DOOR** Gina Wilkins
**A RANCH FOR SARA** Sherryl Woods
**RUGRATS AND RAWHIDE** Peggy Moreland
**A FAMILY WEDDING** Angela Benson
**THE WEDDING GAMBLE** Muriel Jensen

# JASMINE CRESSWELL

**Internationally-acclaimed Bestselling Author**

# SECRET SINS

**The rich are different—they're deadly!**

Judge Victor Rodier is a powerful and
dangerous man. At the age of twenty-seven,
Jessica Marie Pazmany is confronted with
terrifying evidence that her real name is
Liliana Rodier. A threat on her life prompts
Jessica to seek an appointment with her
father—a meeting she may live to regret.

**AVAILABLE IN PAPERBACK
FROM JULY 1997**

# Bureau de Change

How would you like to win a year's supply of Silhouette® books? Well you can and they're FREE! Simply complete the competition below and send it to us by 31st January 1998. The first five correct entries picked after the closing date will each win a year's subscription to the Silhouette series of their choice. What could be easier?

| 1. | Lira | Sweden | ___ |
| 2. | Franc | U.S.A. | ___ |
| 3. | Krona | Sth. Africa | ___ |
| 4. | Escudo | Spain | ___ |
| 5. | Deutschmark | Austria | ___ |
| 6. | Schilling | Greece | ___ |
| 7. | Drachma | Japan | ___ |
| 8. | Dollar | India | ___ |
| 9. | Rand | Portugal | _4_ |
| 10. | Peseta | Germany | ___ |
| 11. | Yen | France | ___ |
| 12. | Rupee | Italy | ___ |

C7G

**Please turn over for details of how to enter...**

# How to enter...

It's that time of year again when most people like to pack their suitcases and head off on holiday to relax. That usually means a visit to the Bureau de Change... Overleaf there are twelve foreign countries and twelve currencies which belong to them but unfortunately they're all in a muddle! All you have to do is match each currency to its country by putting the number of the currency on the line beside the correct country. One of them is done for you! Don't forget to fill in your name and address in the space provided below and pop this page in a envelope (you don't even need a stamp) and post it today. Hurry competition ends 31st January 1998.

## Silhouette Bureau de Change Competition
### FREEPOST, Croydon, Surrey, CR9 3WZ
EIRE readers send competition to PO Box 4546, Dublin 24.

Please tick the series you would like to receive if you are a winner
Sensation™ ❏  Intrigue™ ❏  Desire™ ❏  Special Edition™ ❏

Are you a Reader Service™ Subscriber?     Yes ❏    No ❏

Ms/Mrs/Miss/Mr_____
                                              (BLOCK CAPS PLEASE)
Address_____

_____

_____ Postcode_____
(I am over 18 years of age)